THIS COLD NIGHT

THIS COLD NIGHT

by Erica Schaef

Edited by Carrie Allison-Rolling
Proofread and copy edited by Stephanie Ellis
Formatted by Stephanie Ellis

Cover illustration and design by Elizabeth Leggett
First Edition: December 2022

ISBN (paperback): 978-1-957537-09-2
ISBN (ebook): 978-1-957537-08-5
Library of Congress Control Number: 2022950748

BRIGIDS GATE PRESS
Bucyrus, Kansas
www.brigidsgatepress.com

Printed in the United States of America

For Xander and Rowan, with all of my love, always.

Content warnings are provided at the end of the book

PRELUDE

"This cold night will turn us all to fools and madmen."
-William Shakespeare, *King Lear*

Her skin was like wax, cracked and so pale it was almost translucent. Tiny purple and pink capillaries spread out underneath in a mangled web, the blood within them coagulated and still. There was no color in her sunken cheeks, no hair to cover her smooth scalp.

The chemotherapy treatments had taken so much from her that she wasn't even recognizable by the time death had finally come. This wasn't her. The thing before me was just a shell.

I had to turn away. The funeral parlor smelled like formaldehyde vaguely disguised with floral perfume. *She doesn't belong here.*

Chapter One

"What, is it like an allegory or something?"

Finn looked up from his drink, his face bathed in the amber glow of firelight. "The fuck is an allegory?"

"The text she sent you, these emojis … do they have some hidden, special meaning for the two of you?" I handed the cell phone back to him.

"An umbrella and a knife? No, no *special meaning*. Unless she wants to stab me in the fuckin' rain or some shit." He was swearing a lot, a sure sign that the whiskey sodas he'd been downing over the last hour and a half were finally starting to take effect.

I shrugged. "Probably a mistake then. Maybe she didn't mean to text you at all."

"Come on, Shell-bell. She breaks up with me out of the fuckin' blue, doesn't talk to me for months, *months*, then just happens to send this shit on the day of my mom's funeral?" His brow wrinkled over his dark eyes as he returned the phone to his pocket.

Not exactly out of the blue, I refrained from saying. Actually, I remembered being surprised his relationship with Nia had lasted as long as it did. Instead of voicing this, I simply put my hand on Finn's shoulder and gave it a gentle squeeze.

He covered my hand with his, and we sat in silence for a while, watching the fire burn in the grate across from us, warming the oversized room. It was an immensely comfortable place, cozy despite its spaciousness.

"Thanks, Shell-bell," he said after a few minutes, removing his hand from mine to tug lightly on the braid at the back of my neck, like he had done so often when we were children. Chills ran down my spine at the contact. "You're always here for me. Christ, can you believe we're going to be thirty?"

But I wasn't listening anymore, not really. I had gone rigid, and a sudden cold sweat was dampening my neck and palms. My heart skipped in my chest the way it always did when I was anxious. "Uh, excuse me for a sec ... bathroom." I pressed one clammy palm to the decorative scarf wrapped over the top of my head and stood. My shoes sank into a decadent Persian rug.

Finn tilted his head to the side, and made to stand as well. "You okay, Shell? You're really fuckin' pale ..."

I was already at the doorway. "Fine. I'll be right back."

Without waiting to hear Finn's reply, I stepped out into the hallway, keeping my hand pressed tightly to the scarf as I moved. I winced at the loud clicks my kitten heels made against the hardwood floor. A heavy pulse beat against my throat. I made the conscious effort to slow my pace to a more natural one, forcing myself to breathe. I knew my way, at least. The brooding country mansion was almost as familiar to me as my own childhood home.

Large oil paintings lined one side of the hallway, their usually benign subjects menacing in the partial darkness. One in particular, of a young girl holding a bouquet of drooping bluebonnets, served to set my nerves even more on edge, if that were possible. Her eyes, round and periwinkle, seemed to twinkle in a conceited way, as if she held some damaging secret, and one corner of her cupid's bow mouth was curved up at the end into a malicious grin. I turned my gaze away, looking instead toward the long, narrow windows punctuating the wall opposite.

Snow had begun to fall, and was coming down so thickly that it appeared as if someone had hung sheer white curtains over the outside of the windowpanes. I couldn't even make out the stone water feature I knew to be situated at the center of the courtyard beyond. Maybe that was a good thing, considering. The aged fountain was still the clear effigy of what I took to be an angel, pouring water into a basin, but which had always looked more like a great, winged demon to me. When we were children, Finn and I used to laughingly refer to it as *The Pterodactyl Man*, partly because of its beak-like mouth, but it had always creeped me out.

To my other side was a long, oval mirror. Its intricate silver frame glistened in the dim light, catching my eye. An empty feeling expanded within me at the sight of the familiar object. Alice Ferguson, Finn's mother, had inherited it from her parents. I remembered well the way she used to admire and care for it. Every week she would wipe down the reflective glass with a soft cloth, humming as she did so. Then she would polish the delicate frame, meticulously covering every grooved surface of it. The ache, the void I felt looking at the dust-coated glass and silver, was more than I could bear. I kept walking.

When I finally reached the large oak door that led into the bathroom, the arches of my feet were aching. Once inside, I stepped out of my shoes and carried them over to the marble sink. I put them down on the counter, watching my reflection in the mirror hanging above. Finn had been right, I did look pale, and that was saying something. Despite my naturally jet-black hair, my complexion was as white and freckled as everyone else's on my fully Irish father's side. *My natural ... hair.*

Gingerly, I removed my hand from the silk fabric of the scarf, turning my head slowly from side to side. Nothing looked out of place. I reached behind me for my braid, bringing it over one shoulder. It rested there unremarkably. I tested the scarf next, but it was still securely pinned in place. Everything was fine. Finn's gentle pull on the braid had not been enough to disrupt a single hair. I sighed.

The tips of my fingers tingled in a sickeningly familiar way. I pressed them together, continuing to stare at my reflection. My skin prickled, rising into anticipatory goose pimples as I imagined reaching up to slip my fingers under the scarf, under the faux hair, under the wig cap, to where an immense pressure was building under my scalp, and allowing them to do what they ached to do ...

A booming noise, so loud it shook the walls and floor, tore me from my thoughts. I gripped the counter, my knuckles blanching white. Distant screams reached my ears from one of the house's outer rooms. Several of the funeral guests had followed us back from the graveyard after the burial, bringing with them various food items to leave with Finn. Apparently, they were still in the house, even though Finn had managed to disentangle himself from their consolatory embraces and shoulder pats nearly two hours ago. He had dragged me along with him into what used to be his father's study, where he had proceeded to raid the liquor cabinet. We had remained there ever since, or rather, until I had gone to the bathroom. I let out a long breath.

In the next instant, the light went out, blinked back on for a fraction of a second, then went out again. Everything was pitch black. More distant screams sounded. The lights had gone out all over the house. *Maybe a transformer had blown somewhere nearby*, I thought. That would explain the booming sound.

I groped around in the darkness for my purse, intending to use the flashlight feature on my cell phone. My fingers closed over one of the kitten-heeled pumps on the counter in the exact moment I realized I'd left my purse, cell phone and all, back in the study.

Get it together, Rachelle.

Surprisingly, the deafening sound and the power outage combined had not rattled me as much as a single tug on my braid had. I left the shoes where they were and turned in the direction of the door, putting my arms out in front of me as I walked. My hand had just found the handle, when I heard the sound of footsteps in the hallway beyond. I pushed the door open, expecting to see Finn.

Instead, I found myself face-to-face with a toad-like woman holding a long wax candle. Her bulging eyes met mine over the dancing flame, and I couldn't repress an astonished yelp.

"Sorry, Aunt Theodora. You startled me."

The elderly woman blinked once, her wrinkled features unchanged in the wake of my exclamation. She wasn't really any relation to me. A great-aunt of Finn's, she had been toted out to the funeral service by her daughter, Eloise. I had always referred to her as Aunt Theodora, because Finn did.

"Sorry, dear." Her high-pitched, sing-song voice was a stark contrast to her batrachian appearance. "We the dead tend to have that effect on the living." Her expression remained placid as she spoke.

I was used to disquieting comments from Aunt Theodora. She had, ever since I could remember, suffered from the singular delusion that she was dead. The doctors had a name for it, *Cotard's Syndrome*. Apparently, it was a very rare psychiatric disorder, diagnosed in only a handful of cases internationally. Doctors had a name for my condition as well, *Trichotillomania*. It wasn't so rare.

"Erm, the power's gone out." I gestured unhelpfully at the darkness around us, unsure of how else to change the subject.

"Yes, I know, dear." She held up her candle as if to say, *obviously*.

"Right." I smiled.

I was spared from any further attempt at conversation by the appearance of Eloise in the hallway. She held the stem of a flashlight in one well-manicured hand. The beam of it shone directly at my eyes as the middle-aged woman hurried toward us.

"Mom, I told you to wait for me," she scolded. "You shouldn't be wandering around in the darkness like this."

Theodora's toad eyes blinked up at her. "And I told *you* I needed to use the toilet." The loose skin underneath her chin quivered as she spoke.

Eloise shook her head in a clear display of exasperation. "I was getting a flashlight. Here, give me that candle before the wax melts and burns your hand."

Theodora shrugged and handed over the candle. "Hot wax wouldn't hurt a corpse," she mumbled.

"Yeah, well I've never known a corpse who needed to use the toilet either, so," Eloise snapped.

Theodora flushed red, her jaw set in anger. "I'm a ..."

"Special case, I know, I know. Go on then, use the toilet, Patient Zero." Eloise held out the flashlight to her mother.

Theodora jerked it from her hand, and I had to bite my cheek to keep from laughing at the string of sing-song curse words that emitted from her as she waddled past me. Eloise stood frowning at the long candle she now held.

"I'll take it," I volunteered. "The candle. I don't have a light."

Eloise's green eyes snapped up to meet mine. Then they swept up to the scarf in my hair, and down until they landed on the toes of my bare feet. I resisted the urge to squirm under the scrutinizing gaze. "Rachelle Collins," she said, aware that I stood in front of her. "Here."

I accepted the candle from her, watching the way her arms closed over her chest once she was free of it.

"You should come to the study, you and Aunt Theodora, once she's done. Finn has a nice fire going in there."

"Alright." Eloise nodded curtly. "We'll get the others and be there shortly."

I smiled, wondering how many others there were.

Finn was half-asleep when I returned to the study. Noticing my entrance, he sat up a little in his chair. "Hey, what's with the candle? Power go out?" He stretched his arms out comfortably in front of the fire.

"Yes, did you not hear that huge boom?" I resumed my seat on the chair next to his, digging in my purse for my cell phone.

"Yeah, I wondered what that was," he answered lazily. "Want a drink?"

"No, and you'd better slow down. We'll have company soon."

"Fuck. Who?"

"Aunt Theodora, Eloise, and I don't know who el … no! It's dead. How can it be dead? It was at like 80 percent!" I held the power button at the side of cell phone down one more time, but the screen remained black.

"Relax, Shell-bell. You can take mine." Finn reached into his pocket, and tossed me the phone.

"Thanks. I thought I could use the flashlight to …"

"What?" he prompted at my sudden pause.

"Yours is dead too," I whined. That was less of a surprise, Finn never kept his phone charged. "Owwe!" I screeched, dropping the candle I'd been holding to look down at the lump of crimson wax already starting to harden over the sensitive skin between my thumb and forefinger.

"What? Shit." Finn stamped out the still-burning candle, which had begun to singe the Persian rug in front of the fireplace.

"Sorry." I grimaced. "Forgot I was holding that."

My stomach twisted as I remembered how much Finn's mother, Alice, had adored the Persian rug. Even just thinking of her made my heart ache. It was something I avoided, especially around Finn. He must have been thinking along the same lines, because when I looked up at him, I noticed a glassiness to his eyes that hadn't been there before. Neither of us said anything.

We were joined a short time later by Aunt Theodora, Eloise, and Finn's uncles: Paul and David. There was also a distant cousin named Lucas whom I had never met before. Apparently, the young man was the estranged son of Finn's third or fourth cousin, Owen Ferguson. Finn had only met him that day as well, and had remarked to me how strange he found it that previously unknown relatives seemed to have materialized into existence at the news of his wealthy mother's death. It did not appear the other guests knew much about the young man either, as he always seemed to be hovering on the periphery of the group.

The seven of us sat in chairs and sofas around the fire, eating cold casseroles and blackberry pie. Uncle Paul, a tall straitlaced man in a simple, yet immaculate, suit, told stories about his sister Alice as a child, detailing the way she used to bat her eyes and use her dimpled smile to get them out of trouble. We were all genuinely entertained by this, and it was good to hear the sound of Finn's deep rumbling laughter again. I sat back in my chair, with a full belly and warm feet. Paul's voice was monotone, soothing, and I wasn't even aware of drifting off.

The next thing I knew, large hands were shaking me awake. "Finn, wha—?" I groaned.

"Come on," he whispered into my ear. "Get up. I need to show you something."

I wanted to refuse, to fall back into my comfortable sleep, but something in his voice prompted me to obey.

"Here's your coat." He pushed the plush faux-fur into my lap, then placed a pair of wool socks and well-worn snow boots at my feet

"We're going outside?" I asked groggily, noticing for the first time the dusting of snow on his coat and hair.

"Yeah. You know that Lucas kid, my fourth cousin or whatever?"

I nodded, thinking of the skinny, sickly-looking young man I had met for the first time that evening.

"Well, after you had nodded off, everyone else decided to stay the night here, too, because of the snowstorm … kind of just invited themselves, actually. Anyway, I noticed him acting weird as fuck after he thought everyone else was asleep. Uncle David and I were still in this room with him and you, but Uncle David was snoring away, like he is now, and I must've seemed like I was sleeping too. Lucas looked really closely at your purse, and even opened a couple of the drawers in Dad's desk. He didn't take anything, I would've stopped him if he'd tried, but I wanted to see what he was going to do."

I kept my eyes on his as I pulled the wool socks up over my feet, wondering just how close he'd let this Lucas get to my purse, to me.

"He left the room, and I waited a few seconds to follow him out. I lost him once he got outside, but I saw he was walking toward the cars and figured he was going to try to break into one. When I got down to the cars, there was nothing there. No sign of him. I looked around for a while, but nothing. Then, when I was coming back up to the house, I noticed something on the snow, there wasn't much of it, but it looked like blood."

"Oh," I gasped. "Is he hurt?"

"I don't know. He wasn't there, and there was just that little bit of blood … or whatever it was. After I came in and saw he wasn't back yet, I decided to get in touch with the police, in case the kid *was* hurt or something. It's freezing out there. Anyway, I tried the phone … there's still the landline in the kitchen, but it's dead. I'm sure no one else here has a cell phone, except maybe Lucas. Uncle David's made it his mission to scare everyone in the family off them. Says the government uses them to track us all, and they cause cancer and some other bullshit." He rolled his eyes. "Anyway, I want you to look at whatever it is out there on the snow, maybe it's nothing, but it'll be covered soon."

I nodded, intrigued despite myself. "Alright."

We crept from the room as silently as we could manage in our squeaking boots. Finn walked in front of me with a flashlight once we reached the hallway. I looked to the windows again. The snow was still falling, but not quite as heavily as before. I could make out the shadowy form of the fountain. Judging the height of the snow compared to it, I guessed a good few feet had accumulated from the sudden nor'easter.

"Pterodactyl Man," I whispered, grinning. I felt almost like a kid again, sneaking around the old house at night.

"Christ, I'd almost forgotten we used to call it that." Finn snickered.

By the time we had reached the front door, the novelty of our midnight expedition had worn off and I was thinking longingly of my chair by the fire. Outside, the frigid wind whipped my face and hair, causing my eyes to blur with tears.

"How do you expect me to see anything in this?" I complained.

"Come on, it's not far," Finn called over his shoulder.

I trudged behind him in my oversized boots, making my strides uncomfortably long so that my feet would fall in his tracks. The snow was deep but hard and well-packed, otherwise it would have been impossible to move in.

We went on for a minute or so before Finn stopped to shine the light on a patch of stained snow in front of him. I made my way to his side, sweating with the effort despite the cold. I bent down to look at the partially-covered stain. A distinctly metallic scent was carried on the raging wind.

"Definitely blood," I said, straightening. "But, like you said, there's not very much. Could belong to an animal or someth—"

"What the fuck is that?" Finn interrupted.

"What?" I looked around us in alarm.

"Shh … listen." He grabbed my arm to make me still.

At first, I couldn't hear anything over the howling wind. Then, a low groaning reached my ears.

"Sounds like an injured animal," I whispered uncertainly.

"I'd better go and make sure. Stay here."

I watched him walk in the direction of the pine forest at one edge of the property, not all that keen on being left alone. The groaning hadn't stopped, but it seemed to be growing weaker. My fingers were reaching up toward my hair on their own accord. I tightened them into a fist, even as the prickling sensation returned to my scalp. The urge to pull was almost unbearable.

"Oh, fuck! What the fuck!"

Finn. Without pausing to consider the idea, I hurried toward the sound of the familiar voice, nearly losing my boots to the relentless snow in the struggle.

"Finn?" I called out blindly.

"Christ, oh fuck!"

I kept moving, battling the cold wind until I saw the form of my friend, kneeling in the deep snow in front of … something.

Gasping and exhausted, I finally reached his side.

"Finn, what is it?" I asked, but part of me already knew.

The groaning was just in front of us. I followed the beam of Finn's flashlight to the contorted form of Lucas splayed upon the ground. The tortured sound was coming from him.

"Oh my God!" I stepped forward as the wind seemed to tear the breath from my lungs.

Congealed blood mixed with melting snow covered his chest and abdomen. I knelt down beside his head. "You're going to be alright, Lucas. We're going to get help." My voice was dry and shaking.

One last, ragged breath escaped him, then he went completely still.

"Finn, we've got to get help. Try your truck, walk if you have to. He's dying."

Finn rose without a word and began to walk in the direction of the parked cars, leaving his flashlight aimed at Lucas. I knew it was hopeless. No one was going to get anywhere in this storm. It didn't feel right not to at least try. Turning back to Lucas, I did the only thing I could think of. Moving so that my hands were positioned over his chest, I attempted to do compressions. I nearly lost consciousness when my hands pushed down on the fabric of shirt, then sunk to come in contact with something warm and wriggling.

Bracing myself, I lifted the shirt. What I took at first to be a large mass of pink, fleshy snakes caused me to shriek. It took a breathless moment for me to realize what it actually was: intestines, still peristaltic. Lucas's torso was one massive hole, with bones and organs exposed to my view. I retched as my eyes took in the shredded diaphragm, the swollen, purplish lungs. What in the hell could have done this him?

I was choking on a sob when something very loud and very near caused me to go rigid ... a sound like the beating of gigantic wings just above me.

CHAPTER TWO

Pterodactyl Man? That was my first absurd thought. My second was of the Great Horned Owl I'd seen once while camping. It had a wingspan of only a few feet, though, and there was no way it could have done this to Lucas.

When I finally turned to look up, I could see nothing beyond the falling snow except for darkness. I could still hear the wings, however, beating somewhere just out of sight.

My hand went automatically to my scalp, and for the first time in a long time, I did not resist the urge to reach up. My fingers brushed beneath the wig cap to where pressure built under my skin, above my right ear. Finding a thick hair right at the center of the pressure, I closed my thumb and forefinger around it and pulled. The pressure was immediately relieved. I closed my eyes, trying not to hear the wings, trying to focus on the surge of endorphins produced by the pulling. When I felt I had the strength to do it, I stood, then ran. My eyes closed, my heart beating wildly in my chest, I pumped my legs through the snow, not stopping when one boot stuck and was pulled off. I kept moving, impervious to the cold.

The sound of wings came closer, closer, until the wind from them felt more powerful than that of the storm. There was a deafening *swooshing*, then what sounded like the crunching of bone. My body was numb, whether from the freezing temperature or abject terror. I collapsed into the hard snow, unable to keep myself upright any longer. I heard a massive beating sound right behind me. Snow was being blown in drifts by the resulting force of wind. Then, the sound of them slowly began to grow fainter; higher.

Something fell onto my cheek, something warm, and wet. I remained motionless until the sound of beating wings disappeared altogether, and only the howling wind of the blizzard remained. I opened my eyes and put my hand over the thing on my cheek, flinging it to the ground beside me. A chunk of flesh, wrapped in a torn piece of fabric matching that of Lucas's shirt, landed with a sickening thud on the freshly fallen snow next to my face.

I let out an involuntary whimper, pressing my lips together in an effort not to scream. Fine blond hair was still attached to the skin, droplets of snow beginning to cling to the individual strands. It wasn't possible. *This wasn't possible.*

I didn't want to move. As snow continued to fall onto me, I wanted to disappear underneath it, where that ... *thing*, whatever it was, couldn't find me. I had to force myself to stand again. Both of my feet were numb, even the one still clad in its snow boot. Whilst I walked with my eyes open, it was impossible to properly orient myself in the snow-blanketed darkness.

I kept going forward. My lungs hurt with every forced breath of air. Tears and snow drenched my face and neck, and my hands were sticky with Lucas's blood. It was like moving through a muddled nightmare. I couldn't make sense of anything.

A faint light appeared in the swirling distance, giving me something upon which to focus. I couldn't tell how far the yellowish orb was from me, but I knew I wanted to be closer, I *had* to be closer. To some primordial part of my brain, light meant heat, and my body needed heat. I was led along by pure instinct, as the more cerebral, conscious part of me began to slow and surrender.

The light was small, even as I drew nearer to it, and low to the ground. My breath caught as my sluggish brain recognized it for what it was. A flashlight—Finn's flashlight—the one he had left behind with me when he'd gone for help. It was lodged against the side of a tree, its former position having apparently been disrupted by the snowdrifts caused by the beating wings. Its presence at my feet meant I had likely walked in a circle. I listened, turning my face up toward the sky. Though there was no sound of wings, the strong scent of pine needles confirmed my fear: I had been moving away from the house, away from any hope of safety. I was near the forest at the edge of the estate. My shoulders sagged at the realization, and my eyes welled with tears. A strangled sob escaped me, and the simple act of standing became too much. My legs began to buckle and sway, I could feel myself starting to collapse. Strong arms appeared around my waist, keeping me upright.

"Shell? What?" Finn's voice was strained.

A sliver of relief cut through my confusion. Finn was alright. "Need to get inside," I choked out. "Need to get away from it … need to go."

"Where's … what happened to Lucas, to his … body?"

"That thing, that winged *thing* took it. Get us to the house, *please* Finn. Please, before it comes back." My voice trailed off into a whimper.

"What comes back? What the fuck did this?" Finn's voice was trembling, too, as he reached to pick up the blood-spattered flashlight.

"We need to go," I said with all of the emphasis I could manage. Still, my words were hardly audible over the blowing wind.

I took a shaking step, then was grateful to be lifted up against Finn's warm chest. He cradled me like a small child, which was exactly how I felt in that moment: a fragile, frightened little girl. It was an all-too familiar sense of being. And there was Finn, as always, left to pick up the pieces. I didn't want to think of that now, didn't want the memories of a neglect-filled childhood to become the last I might ever have.

"You couldn't get anywhere in your truck," I whispered. It wasn't even a question.

"My truck wouldn't start."

Dead phones, dead truck, dead everything. I squeezed my eyes shut.

I knew we had made it inside when the wind no longer whipped against me. It was still very cold, but the painful tingle in my toes and fingers was a sign feeling was returning there at least. I opened my eyes again. The flashlight shone on the walls around us, orienting me to our position.

When we reached the long hallway that led toward the study, I couldn't resist the urge to look for the fountain. Ridiculously, I wanted to make sure it was still there, that it hadn't somehow come alive in the night. I could only see the shadowed form of it through the window in the darkness, still a chill ran down my spine. I turned my head, catching sight of the girl with the bluebonnets over Finn's arm. She seemed even more *alive* than she had earlier, as though at any moment she was going to toss her hair back carelessly and laugh at the trembling mess of a woman before her. My eyes flitted to the next painting in the row as Finn continued to convey my limp body forward.

A beautiful young woman with flowing black hair and a lilac-colored dress was perched on a wooden swing. Cherry-blossoms framed her face, their petals caught in mid-cascade all around her. There was a confident tilt to her chin, but her smile was friendly, her brown eyes warm. I felt a little calmer somehow, looking at her. It was almost like peering into a memory, one tinged with sweetness and warmth. She was familiar to me somehow, and the sight of her reassured me in some small way.

When we reached the door of the study, Finn put me down, holding on to my shoulders as I gained my bearings.

"Shell-bell." His eyes flitted up to the scarf on my head. "Your hair."

I felt myself flush as realization dawned. I had displaced my wig, the cap, everything, outside when I had given in to the urge to pull. I hadn't bothered to put it right, hadn't even thought to. That meant at least a portion of my patchy scalp was visible to his eyes. From the concern on his face, I could guess what Finn was thinking. *Sickness. Something bad. Cancer.*

My palms were brown with Lucas's blood. I wiped them on my clothes before reaching for the scarf.

"I'm not sick. Not like *that* at least. Not what you're thinking"—I shook my head—"Finn, what the hell happened out there?"

Finn only frowned.

I couldn't keep the tears back any longer but wondered at how I could still possibly have any left to cry. "I don't know what's happening here. I'm scared, so scared," I blurted.

He nodded, still gripping my shoulder. "It's alright. Come in by the fire, get warm, and tell me exactly what you saw out there."

Uncle David woke as we entered the room, his eyes wide with alarm as Finn put me down in front of the fire.

"What's happened to her?" Uncle David straightened up.

"She's alright," Finn assured him. "But Lucas, that young man that was here …"

I shuddered and Finn stroked my back.

"He was attacked by something," he continued. "Do you know what relation he is … was …?"

"*Was* … you don't mean?" Uncle David frowned.

"He was killed, yes," Finn answered quickly.

"Dear God! Have you called 911?"

Finn shook his head. "Landline's not working, and our cell phones are dead."

"We will bring him inside at least …"

Finn shook his head again. "His body isn't … we wouldn't be able to."

My stomach twisted.

Uncle David gulped. "What did it?"

"I don't know," Finn answered. "Do you know who was with him at the funeral? Who his close family members are?"

"I think he was one of Casey Victor's. My second … no … third cousin, Casey, he died some years ago now, had a whole slew of illegitimate kids, in addition to the five or six with his wife. Lucas is supposedly the son of one of the illegitimates, not sure which, so Casey's grandson. Never met him before today. Eloise and Peter didn't seem to know him well either."

Finn nodded. "Alright. I'm going to have everyone come down here again. Stay here with Shell please, Uncle David. I'll be back soon." He patted my shoulder.

A short time later, Eloise, Aunt Theodora, and Uncle Paul had joined us in the large room. I told, as best I could, everything that had happened out in the snow.

Eloise gasped as I described it. "Why haven't the police been called … an ambulance … something?"

Finn explained patiently about the phones again, and stated he doubted an ambulance could have made a difference anyway.

"Surely, we could go for help?" Eloise insisted.

Finn told her about his truck being dead, and this prompted both Paul and Eloise to want to go outside and check their own vehicles, despite my vehement protests.

"Don't worry, I'll take one of Sam's old pistols with me," assured Paul. "Whatever it was that attacked Lucas, some predatory fowl, I expect, will have a bullet to contend with if it tries anything again."

"No." I shook my head stubbornly. "This was no bird or owl. It was too large, much too large. No bird of prey could have possibly carried Lucas's entire body away like that."

Paul pressed his lips together in a patient way. I knew he thought I was exaggerating. It made me all the more determined to impress upon him, upon everyone, the reality of our situation. "Finn saw that Lucas's body was gone. I saw, well heard, that thing taking it from the ground."

"Yes," Paul said gently, "but you said that the body was already … badly mangled, in pieces really, when you came upon it. Something, a bird of prey as you say, could have attacked the poor young man, then taken his body away … owls … hawks … anything. Sound carries in the snow, and some animals may be hunting at night, even if they usually don't, because of the storm. Maybe a larger animal, like a wolf or coyote attacked him, and what you heard were vultures coming in afterward. Scavenger birds can make quick work of … a body, especially one already—"

"In pieces," I finished, seeing that Paul was reluctant to do so. "No that's not what happened." But suddenly, I wasn't so sure anymore.

Maybe my mind *had* been exaggerating the sound of the wing beats, the gore of Lucas's body. Fear was a powerful thing, after all, and I had been too consumed by it to think rationally. Could it not have been an unusually large and vicious fowl that had done that to Lucas—as Paul suggested? Or more than one of some scavenger bird, and that's why the wings sounded so loud? Sitting there in the well-lit study, surrounded by people, that's what I wanted to believe. Still terrible and heart-wrenching of course, but able to be explained.

"Give me your keys, I'll go out and check your car." Finn held his hand out to Eloise.

She eyed him with her perpetually stern gaze. "No, that's quite alright. I'll manage. I can take a gun as well."

Finn dropped his hand, looking uneasy. "I'll walk with you, then."

"Don't," I said reflexively. "I mean it's not like you would be able to get anywhere tonight. If birds or animals are behaving aggressively because of the weather, why take the chance?"

Eloise leveled me with a cool gaze. "What happened to that boy, Lucas, is going to have to be reported straight away," she said. "If there is a chance to warn someone about this … this bird or wolf, whatever it is, we need to do it. And the police will want to look into the death as soon as possible. We really have no idea what happened to Lucas's body before it was found. There could have been some … some human interference."

My mouth dropped open at this. Was she suggesting that Lucas had been murdered?

"Come on," Finn said, grabbing hold of Eloise's arm. Dad kept his gun safe upstairs."

When the three of them had gone from the room, I turned my gaze to David, who was pacing in front of the fireplace.

"Bet that explosion we heard was an EMP," he muttered, more to himself than to either Theodora or me. "That would explain the outages, the dead truck."

"What's an EMP?" I asked hesitantly.

David stopped his pacing to look over at me, but before he could answer, Theodora's sing-song voice sounded from the corner of the room.

"I wonder if Lucas is stuck somewhere in the house. It never likes to let us go."

23

CHAPTER THREE: *THEM*

It is sweet and fresh and we crave more of it. More of what is ours, more of what belongs to us. More of the blood.

Chapter Four

As I waited for Finn to return, I finally allowed myself to remember Alice.

She had been a godsend in my life. The first time I'd seen her, I was four or five years old, sitting alone in the playground at the town park. Hearing the sound of wheels on pavement, I had looked up. Finn and Alice got out of their car in the parking lot, a powder-blue BMW with cream-colored seats, and I was in awe. Alice was wearing a polka-dot dress and beautiful blue shoes. The sun shone through her brilliantly auburn hair, bringing out hues of chestnut, blonde, and deep red.

Finn was carrying an armful of toys, most of them cars. His hair was thick and the same color as his mother's. He smiled upon seeing me and sat down beside me in the sandbox. I thought his eyes looked like dark honey, the kind I liked to drink straight from the bear-shaped container.

He even let me play with them too. I had never gotten to hold such nice, expensive toys. Finn was kinder than any of the kids at my daycare were to me, never once mentioning my cheap, worn-out dress, which was about two sizes too small. Alice, sitting on a bench nearby, had spoken nicely to me as well, and I thought she was the prettiest lady I'd ever seen. I opened up to them easily, adoring the way they actually paid attention to me when I spoke. That day was the best I could ever remember having, playing and talking with such nice, friendly people. When they had to leave, it was all I could do to keep from breaking down into sobs. Having had that single taste of what a normal, happy family could be like, I desperately wanted more.

When they returned the following week, I thought my heart would burst with excitement. Alice had brought something for me. She called me over and took a brand-new toy out of a bag on the bench beside her. It was a hot-pink Mustang convertible, with headlights that actually turned on, and doors that actually opened. It smelled like a toy store, and was mine to keep, she said, because Finn didn't like pink.

I threw my arms around her neck, breathing deeply the scent of her expensive perfume and smiling so big it hurt. Why wasn't *my* mother like this? Amber Collins had dropped me, her preschool-aged daughter, at the playground and taken off to God-knew-where to be with people I didn't know. It didn't matter she had barely fed me, let me go hungry, left me scared and alone. I was nothing to her—except a bit of extra money from the government.

Alice had brought homemade chocolate chip cookies along with my gift, and Finn and I ate while we played. It was another glorious, happy day. I didn't want it to end. When my mother finally returned a couple of hours later, Alice had introduced herself. Her kind eyes held a shade of disapproval as they studied my neglectful parent. I did not know then how strange it was for a child to be left unattended as I was.

"We have been so charmed by your daughter, Mrs. Collins," Alice told her. "We would love to have her over for dinner and a playdate one night."

Of course, my mother had agreed, anything to be rid of the child who so inconvenienced her for a while. I wasn't complaining. In fact, I was beaming. My heart felt full for the very first time in my life.

Dinner at the Ferguson's quickly became a frequent occurrence. Finn's dad Sam was just as nice as—if somewhat quieter than—the rest of his family.

Finn told me that when they got married, his parents had taken Alice's last name instead of Sam's, and the mansion they lived in had once belonged to her great-grandfather. *How wonderful*, I thought, *to have such deeply embedded roots in a place.*

Alice's gifts had never stopped. They took the form of a new dress here, a pair of suede boots there, and most importantly, I got to spend time with a loving family. I never felt so at home as I did at Ferguson Estate.

Alice had a heart as big as her perfect smile. Even her husband Sam had benefitted from her giving nature. He, as I learned from Finn, had grown up in a rough situation, too, having gone into the foster system at the age of seven or eight. That was part of the reason he had wanted to take the Ferguson name: he had felt no real connection to his own. Alice had been the first person in his life he'd felt had truly cared about him—something I understood perfectly. She was the one to make the house feel like home. She was the rock of her family.

To now sit in the house I loved so much then, and to feel such terror was jarring. As Aunt Theodora voiced her thoughts aloud to David and myself, about Lucas's being "stuck in the house somewhere," I wanted to scream. This was meant to be my safe place.

David looked from her to me, the bewilderment he felt at her statement apparent. He was a stout, broad-shouldered man with red cheeks and a white mustache. His face became easily flushed when he was vexed, as he was now.

"Sorry, what was it you asked me?" He continued to keep his eyes fixed on me, as though quietly dissuading Aunt Theodora from taking any further part in the conversation.

I blinked and let out a hoarse cough, trying to remember what had been said before the theatrical interruption.

"Oh, you mentioned something about ... an EMP I think? That might have caused the power to go out, and Finn's truck not to start. I was wondering what that was exactly."

"Right." His shoulders straightened a little. "Electromagnetic pulse. It's basically a surge of electromagnetic energy. It interferes with all types of electric equipment; anything from cell phones to generators to cars, lights, any type of electric appliance at all."

"What would cause something like that?" I asked.

"That's the big question now, isn't it?" David clasped his hands behind his back and continued pacing. "Could be a natural occurrence, like a solar flare for example, or it could be the result of a man-made weapon. I myself, well, I think it's probably the latter."

"Oh," I said, wondering if there really could be rational explanation for everything I had seen and heard that night. Though that particular explanation was terrifying in its own right. "You think an EMP could be an act of war, you mean?" I coughed.

He shrugged, but his expression was still one of concern. "Well, yes, honestly."

I frowned, considering this. It seemed extreme, especially when the blast and resulting power outage had coincided with a brutal snowstorm. I didn't say anything else on the subject.

It was a tense quarter of an hour, waiting in the study with David and Theodora for the others—Paul, Finn, and Eloise—to return. My chest seemed to grow tighter with every passing moment, making breathing uncomfortable. I remembered, with disturbing clarity, the sight of Lucas, of his body and blood. Finn was out there now ...

Thoughts and ideas swirled and coagulated in my head, getting confused with each other. Could the thing I heard outside really be just some wild animal? Were we under attack from some hostile, foreign army? Was this just a particularly harsh nor'easter? Or, was there something more sinister at play? And, perhaps most resoundingly, was I going insane? Fear was blurring my sense of logic. A need to clear my lungs distracted me from these dizzying questions.

I coughed again. I'd been doing it rather a lot since my prolonged exposure to the cold air. Every so often, I would reach for my phone to check the time, forgetting it was pointless. I paced beside the window, looking out every so often at the relentless snow. Finally, when I heard the first, faint footsteps outside the study in the hall, I rose to my feet, and went to greet the small party.

I burst out into the hallway and ran toward Finn, who looked glum but unharmed. The others, Paul and Eloise, wore unsatisfied expressions as well, yet no one seemed to have been injured. I breathed an audible sigh of relief.

"They wouldn't start?" I asked when I reached Finn.

"No," he sighed.

"None of them!" Eloise's voice was shrill, panicked. "How is it possible?"

"I don't know," I said honestly. "David has an idea about an EMP, I think it is. I don't really understand it fully, but I'm sure he'd explain it again."

Paul shook his head. "He's become so conspiracy-minded. Flooded engines, that's all it is."

Still, I thought to myself, *what satisfying explanation did we have?* Not one of us really knew anything for certain, except that Lucas had been killed, and there was no way for us to get help.

As I turned around to lead the way back to the study, my eyes stopped on something in the courtyard. *Pterodactyl Man.* I could see the outline of the fountain, there was nothing extraordinary about that, but where the water poured from the basin into the fountain base below, I saw a streak of red. The water, having frozen long-since, should not be moving, yet I swore it was, and I swore it was red. I put a hand out in front of Finn.

"Look," I whispered.

But there was nothing to see. Whatever red, flowing water I was sure had been there, was gone. Only the vague, shadowy outline of the fountain met my gaze.

"What? Did you see something?"

"No, nothing." I forced a grin, not wanting to alarm him over my mental state on top of everything else. *Was I hallucinating?*

In the study, I sat beside Finn, listening to Paul and David arguing in muted tones over David's suggestion of an EMP.

Eloise was sitting on the sofa in the corner beside her daughter, speaking sternly, but quietly, so I had to strain to hear what she was saying.

"… really need to stop. I don't want to hear any more about it tonight, it's all too terrifying. Lucas was *killed*. He's dead. That's the end of it. I don't have the energy or the desire to argue with you."

"Of course that isn't the end of it." Aunt Theodora laughed in a musical way. "This house, it pulls us back. Us Fergusons. Haven't you been listening to me? I can't really expect you to understand. *You* haven't died here."

Eloise rubbed her temples with French-tipped index fingers. Whilst she could be short and even condescending toward her mother at times, Eloise had been a constant companion to her since the older woman's minor stroke twenty-something years ago. She took care of Theodora, and so, despite her terseness, I had never been able to fully dislike Eloise. I knew she had sacrificed much of her own freedom to see to her mother's needs, and I respected her for that. That her words could be cutting and her glances cold, did not negate the fact that she loved this family, just like I did.

"You know," Aunt Theodora said thoughtfully, her round eyes even wider than usual. "I think there really *could* be something to this EMP, electromagnetic-whatsit, business of David's. It *is*, I think, some sort of magnetic force that keeps our souls anchored here. I distinctly remember the pull of it, when I died. Just across the way from us in the courtyard, there, you know?" She pointed toward the wall between the study and hallway. "That's where I died."

The nonchalant pronouncement unsettled me. Eloise only rolled her eyes. "That's where you had your stroke, Mom."

Aunt Theodora nodded with enthusiasm. "Yes, exactly. The day I died."

"See there," Paul was saying to David. "You've got poor Theodora going now, with your war theories. Your adding stress to everyone at an already delicate time."

"And I'm sorry for that, but EMPs are *very* real," David said stubbornly. "That's not some fantastic theory of mine either. It's documented science, and ignoring them as a possibility won't help anyone."

"I know they exist," Paul quipped back. "But this idea of it being some sort of government weapon that made the power go out while there just happens to be a raging snowstorm, well"—he huffed—"there's no reason to be spouting such nonsense right now. A young man has been killed for God's sake. Lucas may not have been well known to us, but have some respect. Certainly, now is not the time to be pushing conspiracy theories."

"I've just had another thought," Aunt Theodora broke in, her thin lips curved into a smile.

"Don't you think it's time to get some rest now?" whispered Eloise.

Aunt Theodora ignored her. "Alice."

I felt Finn stiffen beside me at this mention of his mother. My own heart gave a sickening leap.

"Mom, no." Eloise put a hand on Theodora's arm, warning her not to go on.

"No, no," tutted Aunt Theodora. "It's just this. Alice didn't die *here*, you see. She died in that hospital ..."

"Really, Mom," Eloise snapped. "Can't you see how terribly insensitive you're being? We're all here for Alice's funeral ... and now poor Lucas. Stop with this. Now." She cast a glance over at Finn.

"Hush, just let me finish." Theodore reached over to pat her daughter's knee. "Now ... what was it I was saying?" She put a finger to her chin. "I seem to have lost my train of thought."

"Don't worry about it," Eloise told her, obviously relieved.

"No," said Theodora, wrinkling her brow. "I think it was important. Very important, indeed. But it just simply, *poof*"—she moved her hands in a sweeping motion—"right out of my mind."

"Ah, well." Paul smiled at her. "We're all very tired. It's been a terrible day, just terrible. You should really try and get some rest, Theodora. We all should," he added, looking pointedly at David. "We'll be able to get the police in tomorrow, the Animal Control Agent, and whoever else we need to look into ... whatever happened to Lucas."

"Yes, maybe all the cars will just *decide* to start," scoffed David.

"Very likely, actually," countered Paul. "I'm sure the engines and oil have all frozen up in this blizzard. We should definitely see a thawing out tomorrow with the sun."

David did not seem impressed. As he opened his mouth to argue, Finn gave my arm a gentle nudge. "It's getting cold. I'm going to go upstairs to the parlor where Mom kept that damned grand piano. I think there are candles up there, and we could use some more of those. Want to come with me?"

I nodded gratefully, and allowed him to help me up.

"We're going to look for more candles," he told the others, once we were both standing. "I think I know where there are some upstairs, and we will need some more down here before the night's over."

When we had left the room and were safely out of earshot, he turned back to look at me. "Sorry," he said, "I love them all, but I can only take so much of"—he nodded back the way we had come —"*that.*"

I smiled. "Yeah, I mean, I get it. It's a lot. I'm still processing what happened, what I saw out there, what I heard. All that blood. And that … that …" I cleared my throat, telling myself to believe the most logical explanation. I *had* to believe it. What other option was there? "That … bird. And Lucas."

"I know," he said. "That was traumatic as hell. His body, all torn up like that. I don't know how you did it, getting that close to him."

I looked down, thinking of the horrible experience made me want to cry all over again.

A short time later, we reached the polished staircase which wound up to the next story. Two identical wooden cherubs which adorned the banister were just silhouettes.

We ascended in silence, but when we reached the top, Finn headed for his old bedroom.

"What are you doing?" I hissed impatiently. "We're supposed to be getting candles."

"We will. Are you really in a hurry to get back down *there*?" he asked, plopping down on his back on the full-sized bed.

"True," I said, stretching out on the mattress beside him. "I guess there's no rush." I looked up at the circle of light on the ceiling, caused by Finn's flashlight. *It was like a full moon*, I thought, *contained in its very own, smooth sky*. The air in the room smelled like fresh, crisp winter, and I almost felt safe.

I sighed. "I wish this whole night was just a dream."

"I wish these past two weeks were a dream," Finn murmured. "What are we going to do without her?"

I reached over to give his hand a brief squeeze. "I don't know, but we have each other, at least. You'll always have me."

"I know. Thank God." He smiled.

I smiled too, though I knew neither of us looked truly joyful.

"Can I ask you something?" Finn swirled the light in small circles on the ceiling, so that it resembled a giant lightning bug.

"Sure," I said, my muscles relaxing against the soft bed.

"Do you think it's weird that we never, you know, fucked?"

I turned over to my side and slapped him hard on the chest. "*That's* what you want ask me? *Now?*" I shook my head. "And God, no. We're like brother and sister. That would be … I don't know … *wrong*."

His chest rumbled with laughter under my hand. "Yeah, I think of us that way too. Only Nia asked me once if you and I had ever hooked up or whatever. She said it was weird, how close we are. She was like 'I know the two of you have had sex at some point. You're too familiar with each other.' She thought I was lying when I said we hadn't."

I thought about this for a moment, worrying my bottom lip. "I don't think it's weird. I mean, if I were a guy, and we had this exact relationship, she probably wouldn't have had those thoughts."

"If you were a guy, we wouldn't be cuddling in bed together right now." He laughed.

"Shut up." I slapped him again. "We are not *cuddling*." Though I did become aware of how comfortable I was being so close to him.

He was safety, he was family, and it wasn't my fault if other people couldn't understand that. It shouldn't make me feel guilty or weird. I respected boundaries. Even this, lying next to him in bed with no romantic intentions, I would not have done if he were still seeing Nia. I could understand a girlfriend becoming upset over this. But neither Finn nor I had ever given Nia a reason to be jealous.

I took a breath. I was exhausted, scared. Somehow the secret I had been keeping from my best friend seemed to be weighing heavier on my chest than usual. I cleared my raw throat.

"It started when I was eleven, after Mom left, after she'd … *abandoned* me," I started.

Finn did not say anything, although I could feel him tense slightly as he listened.

"Doctors told me later that it was probably a form of self-soothing, but I didn't really know why I did it. It was like I would get this pressure under my scalp and the only way to relieve was to … pull out my hair. I'd pull them out individually, by the root. At first it wasn't noticeable, but then it got out of control. Remember that stupid hat phase I went through in middle school? I couldn't stop myself from doing it, usually I didn't even realize I *was* doing it, it just became a sort of habit. Dad finally took me to the doctor for it, thinking I had some form of alopecia or something. When they told him what it was, *Trichotillomania*, a psychiatric disorder, and suggested therapy, he only laughed. Said he'd be damned if he was going to pay for treatment for something that was 'all in her head,' and that I would just have to 'get over it.' I didn't of course, but I started to use my babysitting money on hats and wigs to cover it. I did end up getting into therapy for it in college, but by then the damage was done. Most of the hair I pulled will never grow back. Anyway, it's something I still struggle with, even now"—I motioned toward the wig above my ear—"obviously."

"Why didn't you tell me?" Finn asked.

I knew he would be kind about this, and for some reason that made me want to cry. "I was embarrassed. Plus, you and your mom were already doing so much for me, letting me stay here all the time. I felt loved. I used to pretend *this* was my actual family, you, your mom and dad, even Aunt Theodora and the rest. I didn't want to lose that, didn't want to become more of a burden than I already was. Some dirty, poor kid from the wrong part of town you just happened to meet at the park one day. I knew I was already a charity case, I didn't want to add to that."

Finn reached out to squeeze my hand. "You *were* family to us, Shell-bell, still are. Mom saw you as the daughter she never had. Nothing could change that shit, not ever. We might have been able to help."

I relaxed a little. "Sorry, we were talking about you and Nia … and the jealousy …"

"That was the least of our fuckin' problems." He sighed. "Nia was a goddamned whirlwind."

"You can be a little chaotic yourself there, Finn," I pointed out.

"Fair." He put his free hand up, surrendering the point. "I don't think we ever really had a chance of making it work, Nia and me."

Though his tone was easy and natural, I knew that Finn still cared deeply for his ex-girlfriend. The way he had over-analyzed her nonsensical text earlier was proof enough of that.

"Well, I don't know. Maybe …" but my words were cut off by an eruption of screams and the sound of shattering glass from downstairs.

Beside me, Finn sat bolt upright. "Shit. What's happened now?"

CHAPTER FIVE: *THEM*

Revitalized, we swell, full and glorious. Full and glorious and ripe and seeing with eyes like those of angels, hundreds of eyes tethered to hundreds of invisible wings, and fluid with vivid sight. Blood runs like fire through us, like fire, manic and free. It sates us, nourishes us, draws us deeper into this place and its illusion of time.

We are watching, waiting, patient, for more. More of the blood, we chant in one voice. Deeper, we sink into this place. More of the blood.

Chapter Six

The first thing I noticed was the dark pool of blood spreading out in trickles on the Persian rug. It stood out violently against the light carpet, crimson on cream. The second thing I noticed was how very dark the room had become. Looking to the fireplace, I saw that only red embers burned there, nearly hidden in a mess of ash. There were black streaks of soot all over the walls and floors, as though something had been dragged away from the hearth.

Eloise's screams filled the room, making it impossible for me to think clearly. My eyes scanned the fireplace: the rug, the walls, the … windows. The large picture window next to Eloise had been completely shattered, apparently from the outside, because tiny shards of glass clung to the curtains and littered the floor below the sill, reflecting the light of the dying fire.

"Uncle David, where's Uncle Paul?" Finn had to practically yell to be heard over Eloise.

I followed his gaze to where David stood next to the fireplace, his arm gripping the ash-laden mantel for support. The older man's face was as white as a sheet as he shook his head. A thick streak of black soot ran down one cheek, blackening the hairs at the edge of his mustache.

"I don't … I don't know what happened. I don't understand …" His voice broke down into trembling murmurs.

Eloise's voice, on the other hand, was growing hoarse from screaming, but still she didn't stop. Only Aunt Theodora remained composed, her hands folded on her lap as if nothing extraordinary had taken place at all. It was disconcerting to see her placid, unconcerned expression among the chaos of the room. It was like looking at a house that had remained singularly untouched in the wake of a hurricane, which had left all its neighbors reduced to a pile of indistinguishable rubble. There was something definitely eerie about the contrast it provided. Still, she might have witnessed something that could lead us toward an explanation.

"Aunt Theodora?" I asked, approaching her slowly. "Do you know … could you tell me what happened? Where did this blood come from?"

Aunt Theodora looked up at me with those large toad eyes. "Dear, I'm afraid you wouldn't believe me if I *did* tell you. So I think I won't bother just now. I'm awfully tired." She gazed straight ahead again, making it clear that the subject was closed. I didn't want to push her, perhaps she was more fragile than she seemed. Avoidance could be an appealing coping mechanism—as I knew.

I looked back at Finn, who was half-carrying his uncle to an armchair across from Aunt Theodora and myself.

Eloise's screaming was becoming overwhelming. I moved to stand in front of her.

"Eloise," I said, as gently as I could.

Her eyes, which had been looking somewhere past me, locked onto mine, and blessedly, the screaming stopped. It took a moment for the ringing echoes of it to die in the room, or perhaps, that ringing was only in my own ears.

"Hey," I went on once I could concentrate. "You're alright. Your mom's alright. Just try to be breathe for me. That's it."

Her chest rose and fell in short, uneven bursts, but her eyes remained locked upon mine. Her typically well-groomed bob was now frazzled, and mascara was running down her typically perfect face. Her eyes were wide and innocent, like those of a child, but there was fear there, so much fear …

"That's it, just keep breathing. It's alright." For some reason, the attempt to calm her was calming me a little as well, slowing my heart rate. There was something about having a task, any task, that kept the rational part of me in control. I reached out to touch her arms, moving gingerly so I wouldn't startle her. I rubbed my hands slowly up and down the fabric of her sleeves. "You're doing so well. Deep breath now."

Her chest expanded as she obeyed my instruction.

"There you go," I encouraged.

I could hear that David was speaking again, but his voice was too low and fragmented for me to understand what he was saying. As much as I wanted to move closer to hear him, I knew I had to stay where I was with Eloise. I thought she might be in shock, and I wanted to keep her as alert and coherent as possible.

Not a full minute later, however, Finn approached us, a fake smile plastered on his face. "Shell-bell, why don't you take Eloise upstairs to the piano parlor?" His voice was sweet, but his eyes implored me to listen. They locked on mine with grave intensity. "I'll help Aunt Theodora. That room has a small fireplace, we can all wait out the night up there."

I longed to ask him what David had told him, but forced myself to concentrate on convincing Eloise to go with me. I held onto her arm, guiding her to the door. David had already gone from the room, I noticed, and Finn was impatient. I could tell by the way he fidgeted and kept glancing over his shoulder at the broken window. The nightmare of finding Lucas in the snow flashed before me, though I'd been working hard to suppress it.

I had allowed myself to be lulled into a false sense of comfort. It had been easy to believe the thing I heard had been a confused and desperate wild animal after all, a freak accident, that my mind had been exaggerating the experience. I had the feeling I wasn't going to be able to cling to that illusion any longer, that whatever had done that to Lucas could not be so easily explained.

Eloise walked beside me as if in a dream. She followed my lead easily, looking forward, but I was sure she was not really seeing what was ahead of us. It was a robotic set of movements, putting one foot in front of the other as I kept my elbow securely hooked under her arm.

The longer we walked, the more agitated I became, anxious to know what had happened in that room while Finn and I were upstairs. Simultaneously, I dreaded hearing about it. That Paul had been killed was a certainty.

Finn was able to light a fire in the upstairs parlor, once we were all settled. It crackled and popped cheerfully in the grate, and the comfortable heat it emitted seemed all wrong somehow, like Aunt Theodora's nonchalance downstairs had been.

I left briefly, to gather blankets and supplies from other rooms to help us get through the night. Upon my return to the room, I locked and bolted the heavy door behind me. David was sitting quietly in an armchair next to Aunt Theodora, his eyes glossed over by an overwhelming combination of confusion and grief. Eloise would not stop staring at the small window at the far side of the room across from her, as though she expected it to burst into pieces at any moment. I had helped her to a chair on the other side of Aunt Theodora and spread a thick quilt over her legs. She had not acknowledged my ministrations, had not seemed to notice that I was even there.

What could have caused that damage to the window downstairs? I thought back to the shards of glass on the fabric of the curtains and on the floor. Something had definitely come in from the outside, something *massive* by the look of the window. Not a bird, not an owl, something bigger than a full-grown man. I cringed at the thought. And Paul, he wasn't there. All the blood on the Persian rug, it had to have been his. Without the distraction of trying to comfort Eloise, I was tormented with the possibilities and the memory of the thing I had heard.

"Finn," I whispered, kneeling beside him in front the fireplace, as he shifted the wood within the grate. "Did David see it? Whatever came through the window?"

Finn glanced over his shoulder toward David, seemingly to make sure he wouldn't overhear us. "No. He said he was standing across from Paul, that they were still arguing. He heard the window breaking, and Eloise screaming. He looked, but he only saw a blur of movement, and Paul was pushed forward. Then there was blood and ash from the fireplace. In the same instant, Paul and whatever had come in through the window, were gone. There was still blood on the floor and glass, and that's it. He didn't see anything else, has no fuckin' idea what happened. Shell, Christ, Shell." His voice shook. My heart sank.

Not only had he had to attend the funeral of his mother, but on the same day, had lost an uncle he'd been close to all his life and had been outside to see Lucas's body. He was also experiencing the same fear and uncertainty I was. We did not even know what the threat looked like, what it was capable of.

"Come here." I put my arms around his neck, burying my face in his chest. "I'm so sorry, Finn. I don't understand what's happening … why it's happening."

"What if it *is* an act of war?" David spoke from his chair behind us. The loud boom of his voice startled me. "What if that thing that killed Lucas, and the thing that took Paul … what if it's some sort of military weapon, a drone of some kind?"

"I don't think so," I said, still holding on to Finn. I half-expected to hear Paul scold his brother about his conspiracy-mindedness. But of course, Paul was not there. I cleared my throat and went on. "When I was outside, I heard something with beating wings, like an enormous bat or something. I don't think it could have been a drone. It just didn't sound in any way mechanical."

"An animal, genetically altered, then? It's a real possibility, isn't it? When you consider the implications of an EMP, I mean, it would make sense. A fully-formed strategy, they've probably released these things all over the country. With the power outages and network breakdowns, they would be deliberately inciting mayhem. What better war tactic could there possibly be? People would be too confused and terrified to realize there even *was* a war, much less be able to do anything about it. Between these animals, whatever they are, and the complete loss of electricity, well we're just sitting ducks, aren't we? Drop a few bombs here and there for good measure, and watch us implode." David stopped to draw a long breath, his eyes coming to rest on the fire rather than on either Finn or myself.

"Really, I don't know," I answered, and that was the truth. My mind was so addled almost anything seemed possible. His rant had been inspired by fear however, and I knew fear could muddle logic with apt skill.

"I don't think this is happening all over the country," Finn said softly. "This can't be fucking happening everywhere. If it were, someone would have done something by now, the government, the military. I think Uncle Paul was right, about the electricity and the cars not starting. It's a winter storm, that shit happens, engines freeze, power goes out. As for the other part, I have no idea. I don't know what would be capable of doing that to Lucas and taking Uncle Paul away so quickly. I think I should go to the police station, though. Tonight, now, and report all of this. We need lights, people. We need to find out what the fuck is going on."

"No," I said, holding onto his shoulders as he tried to stand. "How would you even get there?"

"I'd have to walk," he said simply. He looked at me, trying to communicate something without actually speaking aloud for the others to hear.

"Finn, it's twenty miles into town, there's no way you could get there before morning, and in this weather, you wouldn't even be able to go more than five minutes without starting to feel numb. You'd fall down in a ditch somewhere, no one would know how to find you. And it isn't safe to be outside, you know that. You saw Lucas's body too, same as me. It makes much more sense to wait until morning and see if any of the cars will start."

Finn pulled away from me, rubbing his face with his hands. "I just feel so damned useless," he hissed. "What if Uncle Paul isn't dead? What if he's injured somewhere, and I don't do anything about it?"

"Shh." I gestured toward David and the others behind us, then scooted closer to Finn, so the others would hopefully not be able to hear us. "You saw how much blood was on the floor down there. You know there's no way ..." but I didn't finish. The color had drained from Finn's face. I felt my chest tighten. "Sorry," I hastened to say, "I didn't mean to sound unfeeling. It's just that … well, you can't go out there. Not now, not tonight. Alright? You just can't."

He didn't acknowledge me as he rose to his feet, but instead of walking to the door, he crossed over to look out of the window. I could see his silhouette outlined by one of the candles we had lit around the modestly sized room. My breathing came a little easier now, knowing he wasn't about to walk out to his death.

"Well, aren't we a sullen bunch?" Aunt Theodora chirped. The friendly comment was like a cold slap. But with Eloise too withdrawn into herself to even know what the rest of us were saying, there was no one to correct her crass, insensitive statement. "Cheer up, now. Paul's around somewhere."

David made a show of clearing his throat.

"Uh, why don't we all try and get some rest?" I suggested, sure that none of us would be able to do anything of the sort, except for maybe Aunt Theodora. She needed to be quiet now. I knew everyone's patience was low, our nervous systems overloaded.

"Yes. I think I'll make myself a stiff drink," David said, sounding on the verge of tears. "Anyone else?"

"None for me thanks," I said.

Finn remained silent.

Aunt Theodora shook her head, and Eloise continued to stare blankly at the window, not seeming bothered by the fact Finn now blocked her view of the grounds.

"Very well then," said David, removing a silver flask from his pocket. "To Paul," he said quietly, then put the container to his lips and began to drain the contents.

I stood and moved to a sofa across from Eloise, pulling a thick throw blanket over my body as I stretched out upon it.

David continued to drink from his flask but did not say anything further. He only watched the fire with misty eyes. Finn had gone as quiet as Eloise, but I knew his mind was working relentlessly to find a solution—or at least an explanation for— everything that had happened. He had a heart of gold, just like his mother, and I knew it pained him to see the people he loved suffering like this. It pained me too, made me feel helpless and useless. There was nothing any one of us could do, I knew, except to wait out the night and try to stay safe. I didn't know what the morning would reveal, but I was sure that we were all putting our hope into its bringing an end to the hellish things we'd been subjected to in the night. *Light would bring clarity*, I assured myself. Whatever had attacked Lucas and Paul would have left traces tracks or markings. When the police could be contacted, when they arrived, everything would seem less impossible, less surreal. It would still be a nightmare, a scarring trauma for all who had experienced it, but it would make sense.

A pressure was building at the top of my head, and my fingers itched to relieve it. It amazed me that a compulsion like that could be such an intrinsic part of my brain matter. That piece of me was as ever-present as my personality, my baser urges. Even under the threat of danger, probably especially because of it, my neurons were still transmitting the inane order to pull. Individual hairs plucked out one by one … *one by one.*

Was that what was happening to us? Were we being weeded out, one at a time, for no better reason than it being the whim of whatever was doing this? No, that was ridiculous. But then, what was it? What was this thing? Some savage, violent animal, making especially vicious attacks on humans? Could it be a bobcat? A grizzly bear? It didn't seem likely. What could have broken through the window downstairs with such force, and disappeared out of it again so quickly with Paul? It seemed to me there was little chance it could have been a large cat or bear, but then I knew they could move fast, especially over short distances. I had heard of them attacking people without provocation, unsuspecting hikers or campers. But to break through a window to get to a person seemed especially aggressive. To disappear with a full-grown man's body and leave nothing behind except a puddle of spilt blood seemed impossible. I kept going over it in my head, always coming back to the same question: What other explanation was there?

A sudden, loud *bang* drew my attention to the grand piano at the center of the room. One of the candles we had placed on top of it had fallen over in its brass holder. A second later, a shrill, off-key note sounded from the piano—none of us were near it. I started, sitting upright at the sudden noise.

"Oh." Aunt Theodora chuckled in her high-pitched voice. "You always did love that piano, Paul."

CHAPTER SEVEN

No one said anything for a long while. I forced myself to keep looking at the grand piano, knowing I was being silly for feeling afraid. No ghostly apparition met my gaze, and no other sound issued from the instrument. I focused on breathing, on keeping myself as calm and rational as possible.

Aunt Theodora's words had caused the hairs on my arms to stand on end. I rubbed my hands briskly over them, then curled up under my throw blanket. The room had grown quiet, except for the crackling of the fire. I knew my body was tired, it had to be after everything I had put it through, but there was no way I was going to be able to sleep. Every creak of the house, every gust of wind against the window pane, caused me to start. Eloise's constant, unblinking stare as she looked out into the night was also making me uneasy. *When would she snap out of this daze?* I wondered, hoping it was the temporary result of shock, and not a sign of some trauma-induced psychosis. David was still taking intermittent sips from his flask. His expression was sullen, the light had gone from his eyes. He seemed to be preoccupied with his own thoughts, not once glancing beside him at Aunt Theodora or beyond her to Eloise.

Finn was standing by the window. As I was looking at him, he made a sudden movement, clenching his hand into a fist and hitting the glass. It wasn't a hard blow, but enough to make a sound.

"Fuck, *I just saw it,*" he hissed, then crossed the room to the doorway. His long strides carried him there easily.

"Wait!" I called, throwing off my blanket.

He did not wait, did not even acknowledge that he'd heard me.

I hurried after him, but by the time I gained the corridor, he was already on the stairs.

"Finn!" I ran. "Where are you going?"

"Out there," he called back, not even turning to look at me.

No. What had he seen from the window? Something which had already killed two people. The thought chilled me, but I continued to chase him.

Sam had died a few years ago, and we had only just laid Alice to rest. I couldn't lose Finn, too.

I followed him to the front door, where he pulled out a pistol that had apparently been concealed beneath his clothes. Despite the fact there were no shoes on his feet, he didn't hesitate before plunging out into the cold night.

"Finn!" I yelled, out of breath from the exertion of trying to keep up with him. "No, it's too dangerous!"

Before I had time to fully talk myself out of it. I was following him out the door.

The wind was like ice against my skin. It wasn't snowing anymore. I could see the glow of stars above me in the dark sky as I ran. My socks were already soaked through, my feet aching with cold. "Finn, please!" He had stopped a short distance ahead of me, and was looking up. At the sound of my voice, he turned around.

"Go inside," he ordered.

"Come with me," I pleaded.

"No, *it's here*, I saw it."

"What?" I asked, drawing nearer to him. "What did you see?"

He turned away, looking up toward the sky again. "I saw it from the window, just about here."

"What Finn?" I was close enough now to reach out for him. "What did you see?" I repeated, and touched his arm gently.

He flinched and stepped away. "Go inside, Shell. Now."

I shook my head, though he still wasn't looking at me. "No. Not without you. Tell me what you saw."

"That fucking thing you heard. The thing that took Uncle Paul."

I licked my lips, which were suddenly very dry. "Finn, what is it?"

He continued to look up, his free hand went to his hair, pushing it back from his face. "I don't fuckin' know. It was flying, and so fuckin' big … I don't know. I'm going to shoot it though, I'm going to."

A chill ran down my spine at this. I squeezed my eyes shut, trying to remain composed. I was trembling. I opened my eyes, forcing a deep breath. The air was crisp and fresh, pleasant even. My stomach turned.

"Not tonight," I whispered, reaching for Finn's arm again. "You can go out tomorrow, with more people, more guns, when it's light."

"No." He jerked his arm away from my touch. "I'm going to get the fuckin' thing now. Be quiet."

"Finn …"

He moved so suddenly, I wasn't even aware of what was happening. One second he was beside me, the next he'd maneuvered behind me, his large hand clamped tightly over my mouth. The sound of him cocking the pistol next to my ear kept me from protesting, from moving at all. I remained as still as possible, listening.

I could hear it instantly, the heart-sinking swish of beating wings. As slowly as I could, I tilted my head upward. Finn released his hold on my mouth. He stepped around to stand directly in front of me, pistol raised. I wished that he had a shotgun instead of the short-barreled handgun. *No*, what I *really* wished, was that none of this was happening. Part of me was certain that once I had a clear view of whatever it was that had attacked Lucas and Paul, it would take away some of the fear, some of the unknown.

The sound of wings became louder, nearer. I looked up, directly at the pale, full moon. My breath caught. Something dark and large, very large, passed in front of the stars, the moon, completely eclipsing it. In fact, it eclipsed the sky all around, blocking the light that had been glistening upon the snow. My heart thumped painfully in my chest at the sheer size of the thing. I couldn't even scream.

Finn took a step back, aiming the pistol and firing. Once, twice, three times. The sound of the shots echoed against the snow, the trees. My ears rang with those echoes, aching and throbbing.

"Did you get it?" I whispered. I couldn't make out anything clearly. There was Finn in front of me, and the wet, frozen snow below my feet.

Behind us, someone was calling, "Finn! What are you doing? Come inside."

I turned to see the form of David, standing just outside the house's front door.

"Go inside, now!" Finn yelled back.

There was the sound of the wings again. My insides twisted. It was still alive, still flying. Something black obstructed my view of David, and I couldn't breathe, couldn't move. I caught a glimpse of the wings as they beat: massive, and leathery, like those of a bat. *No, no, no.*

A scream died in my throat as Finn moved forward, firing shots. There was a sickening crunch, and a wet sound, like water gushing to the ground, or—I had a sickening thought—blood.

The enormous black blur of a thing rose up, and then was gone. David was gone. A pool of blood remained on the snow. Spatters of it were everywhere, reflecting the pale moonlight.

Finn was yelling, firing shots into the air until the pistol only clicked, empty of bullets.

My face was numb. My throat hurt. My lungs ached. It took me a moment to realize that I was still screaming. I closed my mouth, thinking of Eloise, and the way we had found her in the study. It seemed impossible, but I needed to think, to move.

"Finn!" I cried, my voice strangled and hoarse.

He turned to face me, then walked toward me so quickly I became impossibly more frightened. It was as if my body had become hyper-vigilant to my surroundings, on constant alert to lurking danger.

"Inside!" he yelled in a booming voice, leaning down so his face was almost touching mine. My ears, already aching, felt as though they were being stabbed.

"Don't." I put my hands over my ears. "Don't stay out here."

"Inside, now!"

I had never heard him yell like that. It was terrifying. I could hear the desperation, the fight for stability, in his words. Finn was always strong, to see him losing control made everything more real to me.

I clutched the front of his shirt, forcing him to stay where he was. "Take me inside," I gasped. I wouldn't leave him here. "Take me inside, Finn. I need you to take me inside."

His eyes, wild with fear and anger, flashed to mine. Without saying anything, he put his arms around me and lifted me from the ground. He put me over his shoulder, so I was looking down at the snow as he carried me. His movements were jerking and ungentle, not like Finn at all.

I knew we were close to the house when I saw blooms of red against the long stretch of pure white. *David's blood.* Then the hardwood floor appeared, and I was placed on my feet. Finn let go of me before I had even regained my balance fully and was hurrying to the staircase.

I stood there like a newborn fawn, unable to force my legs to function. Putting my hand to the wall beside me, I stood for a moment, trying to catch my breath. The feeling began to return to my feet, my stomach muscles unclenched, and I suddenly became aware of how alone I was ... or so I thought.

"I think they're all afraid, Gigi."

The whispered words were coming from the direction of the staircase. I lifted my head, listening.

"Did you see how quickly poor Finn was running?"

I shivered so violently my teeth clashed together. *What the hell?* That voice ... I needed to know who was saying those things. Keeping myself propped against the wall, I began to walk in the direction of the staircase. Everything was cast in shadow, the familiar house had become menacing. I walked until I came to a dark silhouette. Aunt Theodora was standing at the foot of the staircase, her hand resting on one of the wooden cherubs which adorned the ornate banisters. She looked at me as I approached, and I could tell that she was smiling.

"Aunt Theodora," I said weakly. "You should go back upstairs. Something is … something is …" I couldn't bring myself to finish the sentence. I couldn't be the one to tell her what had happened just minutes ago when I didn't even understand it myself.

"Oh, hello dear. Why, you look chilled to the bone. Go upstairs and warm yourself by the fire."

"Uh …" My post-trauma brain had to work hard to keep up with her words. "Who were you talking to just now, Aunt Theodora?" Though the question had issued from my mouth, I was barely aware I'd spoken.

"Just now?" She put a finger to her chin, tapping it lightly. "I don't think I was talking to anyone, dear."

"Who's … I mean … do you know someone named Gigi?"

"Gigi." Her voice softened. "Yes, of course I do …"

The sound of footsteps on the staircase distracted both of us.

"Finn?" I asked, gripping the banister to start climbing.

I had only made it to the fourth stair when he brushed past me. He was holding the pistol, I noticed. Had he gone upstairs only to reload it?

"What are you doing?" I yelled, but of course I already knew. "Stop!"

It took all my strength to run after him. Every breath, every movement, hurt. I managed to run into his back just as he was getting to the door. We both crashed against it, slamming it shut to the cold night beyond.

"Goddamn it, Shell! Take Aunt Theodora upstairs, and stay there. For fuck's sake, just listen to me." Finn turned around, ridding himself of the obstacle that was my unsteady body easily.

I grabbed his arm, digging my fingernails in as hard as I could. He would be next if I let him go out there, I knew it.

"I can't chase you anymore. I can't go out there again."

"Great, don't!" He tried to jerk his arm away, but I held fast, digging into it with my other hand as well. "Get the fuck off me." He brushed my grip away too effortlessly with his free arm. "Stay inside. 'Til morning, 'til help comes. Stay here."

He started to turn away again, and I did the only thing my affected brain could come up with to immobilize him. I clutched his shoulders and brought my knee up hard against his groin. He let out a howl and doubled over.

I wrestled the pistol from his hand, it wasn't hard. He really didn't even seem to realize I was doing it. I walked a few steps to put the weapon on a small table in the foyer, next to an old clock, facing away from us.

When I moved back to Finn, he was looking at me with fury in his eyes. He was still hunched over, so I took the opportunity to push him away from the front door, away from the pistol. I managed to get him almost to the foot of the stairs, where Aunt Theodora was still standing with her hand on the cherub, before he began to straighten.

"What the fuck, Shell?" He looked as if he might hit me.

"Finn, stay," I begged, clutching his hand.

"I can't, Shell." His anger seemed to break, his voice suddenly sad, almost as pleading as my own. "What happened to Uncle David, that was my fault. If I hadn't missed that thing so many times. If I hadn't been so sure that I *could* get it ..."

"No." I took his face in my hands. "Nothing that's happened is your fault. We're all confused. We're all desperate to stop this. You were being protective, proactive. That thing out there it isn't ... isn't ... natural."

He was starting to give in, I could tell by the resigned way he carried his shoulders. Finn was exhausted and, mentally, had reached his limit, just like the rest of us. Except for maybe Aunt Theodora, that was, with her it was almost impossible to tell.

I ran my thumbs over his cheeks, not letting up until I was sure he wouldn't try to go after that awful *thing* again.

"I feel quite wide awake, all of a sudden," Aunt Theodora's sing-song voice rang out next to us. "Is David dead, then?" She asked this conversationally, as though it made no real difference to her, but she thought she would be polite and put the question to us.

"Let's go upstairs," I said, dropping my hands from Finn's face.

"I ..." Finn started, but I didn't let him finish.

I held his hand with mine and pulled him toward the staircase. "This way, Aunt Theodora. We'll help you. Come on." I put out my other arm toward her. She hooked her wrist around it and teetered alongside me, humming serenely as we went.

It was a long walk up the stairs, with one reluctant companion, and another who seemed to be lost in a world all her own. I was anxious to see Eloise, who I thought may have awakened from her shocked stupor, to find herself alone.

When we finally made it to the parlor, I saw that Eloise had not stirred. Her eyes were not on the window, however. Instead, they were closed, and her breathing was rhythmic. I hoped she was getting some much-needed sleep, a thought which made me envious. At least being unconscious would pass the time. I settled Aunt Theodora into her recliner chair while Finn stoked the fire.

"I wish I had something to read," she told me, as I tucked a comforter around the bottom half of her body. "Really, I don't feel at all like sleeping."

"You should try to rest, Aunt Theodora," I told her, although truthfully, she did not seem the least bit tired.

"Oh, I'm afraid that won't be happening. You sleep well, dear," she said, then turned her eyes to the fire, smiling. "You need it."

I didn't know why that last part of our interaction should make me feel uneasy but it did. Everything was putting me on edge. It was like my nervous system had overloaded, and was firing warnings concerning anything I came into contact with.

I stretched out on my sofa again. It was awful to see David's empty chair there, in front of the fire.

Finn stood and I held out my arms to him. "Come here," I said, needing to be sure that he would not try to leave the relative safety of the indoors again. I didn't know what I would do if I didn't have Finn. The thought alone was too much to bear, especially now.

He sank onto the sofa, rolling me so I was half on top of him, with my head on his chest.

"Why don't you take this damned thing off?" he murmured, tugging gently at the scarf on my head.

I shrugged. Truthfully, I didn't know why it mattered. It shouldn't, definitely not in these circumstances. But I knew I wouldn't feel as secure without it, and that was something I couldn't risk just then. "I'm comfortable exactly like this."

He lowered his mouth to kiss the top of my forehead. "I'm sorry, Shell," he whispered. "Sorry for the way I acted downstairs. Sorry that this is happening. Sorry I didn't know about your hair."

I laughed, though his simple words brought tears to my eyes. "I love you, Finn." I couldn't remember having actually said those words to him before, so I wanted to make sure I said them now.

"I love you too, Shell-bell." He rubbed my back with his hand.

"Do you think we're going to be alright?" I asked.

"Yeah," he answered, still stroking my back. "The night isn't going to last forever. It'll be morning soon."

59

CHAPTER EIGHT: *THEM*

Sated, we revel in that which sustains us, which makes us whole, which runs through us in splendorous bounty, overfilling and coursing and reviving that which is eternal. More of the blood, we chant.

CHAPTER NINE

With my head pressed against Finn's chest, I could hear his heart beating. The sound made me think of blood, red and oxygenated, pouring out onto snow, draining life away.

I moved so I was looking at the ceiling, trying to think of anything else. Wracking my mind for a good memory, I caught onto one that had taken place in this house. That was no surprise, all of my most pleasant memories had taken place here.

In this one, I was on a sofa in the downstairs den. Finn was sitting on the floor, his back against my legs, playing some violent video game. We were around ten. It was a rainy summer day.

A copy of Sir Arthur Conan Doyle's *The Adventures of Sherlock Holmes* was open on my lap, and I was reading aloud to Finn. I had reached the part of "A Study In Scarlet" when Holmes and Watson arrive at a murder scene to see that the partial word "RACHE," is written in red on a wall.

"Hey," Finn had interrupted, still busily working his video game controller. "I think it was supposed to say Rachelle. I bet some crazy black-haired girl did the murder."

I nudged him with my knee, laughing. "Oh, shut up," I told him, then resumed my reading. Some of the characters in the story were speculating that the word may have been the start of the woman's name *Racheal.* Finn and I both burst into laughter at this.

"They're getting close," Finn teased, his chest still rumbling with mirth.

Alice had come in then, a tray full of pizza bagels in her arms. Finn jumped up and took a handful of them before she had a chance to set them on the coffee table.

"Careful, honey." Alice smiled. "They're still hot."

But Finn had already plopped one into his mouth, and was resuming his seat on the floor.

"Thanks, Mrs. Ferguson!" I said, smiling widely at her.

"You're welcome, honey," Alice said sweetly.

"Yeah, 'anks, Ma!" Finn garbled, his mouth full of pizza bagel.

Alice shook her head, yet the smile remained on her face. "What am I going to do with you?" But there was pure adoration in her eyes as she looked at her son. True, unconditional love.

My heart had swelled with the knowledge they had welcomed me into their loving world too. Alice's eyes held affection when she looked at me, as well. I loved these people, this place, more than anything else in the whole world.

Lying on the couch with Finn now, I still felt that way, despite everything that had happened in the night.

"Hmm mmm hmm," Aunt Theodora was humming from her chair. It was an eerie, unsettling sound, but I couldn't bring myself to ask her to quiet.

Finn's hand had stilled at the small of my back, he was no longer stroking me in the comforting way he had been. I wondered if he had fallen asleep, though I doubted there was really any chance of that. He had been through so many emotions in this one, single, cold night.

I remembered another afternoon from many years ago, when he and I had been about fifteen. We were in the downstairs den again, but instead of *Sherlock Holmes*, I was reading from Shakespeare's *King Lear*.

"I have no fucking idea what's happening," Finn had said, when I paused near the end to ask him which of the characters he wanted to focus on for our essay assignment. "Who's that one girl? Cornucopia, or whatever?"

"Cordelia." I laughed. "She was the King's youngest daughter, she used to be his favorite, *until* ..." I prompted.

"Until ... she dropped out of school to smoke weed with her stoner boyfriend?"

I rolled my eyes. "Seriously, Finn?"

"Until she took off to Vegas to blow all the King's money on the strip?"

I couldn't suppress a giggle. "Um, no. Anyway, I think the Fool is a really interesting character. I mean it's sort of ironic, that in their interactions, he kind of had more sense than the King. Like Regan's one line … what was it?" I flipped back through the pages. "Oh yeah, here it is. *'Jesters do oft prove prophets.'* I think there could have been a kind of double meaning to that, you know?"

"Uh … what?"

"Like, the line was directed at Albany, about something entirely different, basically saying not to joke around about serious things, what you say might prove true, but it could be alluding to the Fool as well?"

"Um, sure? If you say so."

I ignored him. "Then, in the part about the storm, the Fool says, let me see … here it is. *'This cold night will turn us all to fools and madmen.'* And the King is about to go insane and tear off his clothes and everything. I think there would be a lot to work with, if we did the Fool, and a bunch of other people are probably doing their essays on Cordelia. But we *can* do it on her, if you really want to?"

Finn was stretched out on the floor, tossing a throw pillow in the air and catching it again before it hit his face. "No, let's do your idea."

"You sure?" I asked, watching the progress of the pillow.

"Yea, I have no clue about any of this shit."

"Better not let your mother hear you talking like that," a voice had called from the doorway.

We both looked up to see Finn's dad, Sam, coming into the room. He was holding a large shopping bag in his hand. "Stopped by that new hobby store after work. Found these." He reached into the bag, pulling out one box and handing it to Finn, and then another, which he handed to me. My eyes lit up as I looked at it. It was a scale model kit for a 1967 black Ford Mustang Shelby GT350.

"Oh, it's gorgeous!" I placed the box gently on the couch beside me, and stood to hug Sam.

"Thought you'd like that one," he said, giving me a thump on the back.

"Sick." Finn stood as well. He was holding a kit for a stingray blue Chevy Corvette. "Thanks, man." He threw an arm over his dad's shoulder.

I returned to my seat on the couch, and took the box in my lap, the worn-out copy of *King Lear* forgotten on the cushion beside me. My eyes began to tear as I looked down at the beautiful car. My own father would have never done something so thoughtful. He wouldn't even have any idea what my favorite car *was*, or why. Half the time, I was surprised he even remembered my name. Then there was Sam, who had spent the time to carefully pick out these model kits, and for no other reason than to make Finn and me smile. It made my heart ache.

The memory faded, and I was back in the piano room, listening to Aunt Theodora's humming, and feeling the rise and fall of Finn's chest beneath my head. I tried to focus on the sound of the crackling fire, instead of the strange melody of the humming. It was unnerving, and my fingertips twitched with the urge to pull. My scalp burned with pressure.

"Finn?" I whispered, turning my face to look up him.

"Yeah?" He sounded grim and solemn, so unlike himself. I was selfishly glad that he was still awake too.

"Do you remember when your dad bought those model car kits for us?"

"Hmm?"

"The Mustang and the Corvette. When we were in high school."

"What? I don't know, Shell." He sounded annoyed.

I bit my lip. It had been a very trivial thing to bring up, especially considering all the grief and unwarranted guilt I knew was weighing on Finn's mind.

I had wanted to share with him the joy the memory had brought me, but in hindsight it had been a stupid thing to ask.

"Do you think they felt it?" Finn surprised me with his question.

I had to think for a second. "Felt it? Do you mean …"

He breathed in, I could feel the expansion of his ribs beneath my head. The memory of an exposed ribcage and pink, shining organs in the snow flashed like a bolt of electricity in front of me. Bright blood everywhere, staining my clothes and hands. I blinked, clearing the invisible image of Lucas's body from my mind.

"Uncle Paul and Uncle David. Do you think they felt any pain? I think they probably died instantly, right? Not like Lucas out there in the snow."

I put my arm around Finn's torso, hugging him close. I too, remembered the awful groaning noises Lucas had been making, just before he'd stopped breathing.

"Right," I said, with far more confidence than I felt.

"They probably didn't even fucking know what was happening," he added.

These thoughts had been tormenting him, I knew. He couldn't stand the thought of his family in pain. Neither could I.

"No, they didn't have any idea, it all happened way too fast, just a blur."

He moved his arm, brushing the hair back from his forehead. "God, why? Why is this happening?" His voice was a harsh whisper.

"I don't know Finn, but I do know that *thing*, whatever it is, is not like anything I've ever seen or even heard of before."

"You know," he said after a moment, "I was fuckin' sure that I got it with that second bullet. Do you remember? Before … before Uncle David came out?"

I shook my head, thinking. "I remember hearing the shots, but nothing about the second one specifically. What happened?"

He moved a little underneath me. "Nothing. It was right over us, I could see the outline of its wings and body, so clearly. My first shot might have missed, I was panicked. But that second one, it was aimed right at the center of that fuckin' thing. There's no goddamned way it didn't hit. I even heard an impact, but it must've been the bullet ricocheting off something else, I don't know how. It sounded hard, like metal against cement, or stone. And that thing still flying above us was completely unaffected. I aimed the next one at its left wing, but again, nothing. There should have at least been blood, or a cry, something to show that I'd got it, something to show that it had been injured. But *nothing*. And how the fuck did it do that to Uncle David? Is it something with teeth? Fuckin' what, Shell? I don't think I can keep trying to figure it out … Goddamn I feel like I'm going fucking insane."

I moved so my head was on his shoulder, my fingers stroking his jaw. Aunt Theodora was still humming in her high-pitched way, and that wasn't going to help anyone feel in their right mind. The room, the fire, Eloise—everything served to make our situation seem even more otherworldly than it already did.

"Something *is* definitely unnatural about that thing, Finn. You're not losing it. We just … we just have to make it through the rest of the night. Like you said earlier, it'll be morning soon."

"Yeah, I just … I mean I feel like I should've been able to do something. I can't shake the thought that if Dad were still alive, he would've known what to do, you know? He always knew what to do."

"He would've been so proud of you today, Finn," I said, honestly.

"You don't have to say that—"

"Really," I interrupted, "I mean it. You're so much more like him than I think you even realize."

"Thanks, Shell," he whispered, and I could hear the raw emotion in his voice.

Aunt Theodora's humming stopped abruptly. Its sudden absence was somehow just as unnerving as its constant presence had been.

In the relatively small room, there was a tense and sorrowful atmosphere. It was quiet, almost lonely somehow, as though hollow with the voids left by the people no longer there.

The pressure from earlier now felt more pronounced beneath my scalp. My fingers pulsed and tingled with need. A line from another Shakespeare play, *Macbeth*, seemed to echo in my head: '*By the pricking of my thumbs, something wicked this way comes.*' I shivered, and snuggled more closely to Finn's chest.

"I miss him. Your dad," I said, as much to acknowledge the fact to myself as to Finn. "And *her*. I miss her *so much*." Tears welled over again, though my body was too exhausted to actually cry. "I miss her more than I ever missed my own mother, and I was just a kid when she left. But it didn't hurt like this." I hadn't meant to let all of those things out in front of Finn. It was *his* mother who had been buried that day, he should be the one unburdening himself of his grief, not me. Still, the pain was overwhelming.

There was a loud thump from the outside of the window, as if something had crashed into the pane. It shook the walls before an ear-splitting shriek joined the remnants of the persistent rumble to break the uneasy quiet of the room.

Eloise had gotten to her feet and was staring, white-faced, out of the window. Her arm was held out straight in front of her, her index finger pointing toward the snowy night.

"She saw it," I said, as Finn and I moved to get off the sofa, though no one would be able to hear me over the constant scream that was once again issuing from her.

We were no sooner standing upright than Eloise had bolted to the door, not stopping for breath as she continued her high-pitched wail.

"What the fuck is she doing?" Finn murmured, hurrying to follow her from the room.

I crossed over to the window, to see if I could get a view of the thing that had so recently hit against it with that resounding thud. There was nothing there except the still winter night and its pure, white snow. I watched for a moment, but could detect no movement, no dark shape against the canopy of stars beyond.

"Do you want to know what it feels like to die?" Aunt Theodora's sing-song voice asked from behind me.

I turned around sharply to see her wearing a sweet, questioning smile.

"Wha ... I've ... uh ... got to go find Finn and Eloise. It's not safe to be ... to be ... uh ..." Her toad-like stare, combined with the morose question she'd just asked me were agitating my shot nerves. "Got to go," I said, hurrying to get around her. "Stay here, Aunt Theodora."

"Don't worry about me, dear," she called, as I walked through the doorway. "There's nothing for *me* to be afraid of anymore."

Her words followed me through the upstairs corridor, causing the fine hairs at the back of my neck to stand on end.

I could hear Eloise's scream echoing throughout the house, but it was impossible for me to pin down exactly where it was coming from. It seemed to reverberate from the walls and floor of every room, disorienting me more than the darkness was doing. Long shadows stretched toward me from every direction, like jagged fingers ready to engulf me into their depths.

"Finn?" I called, once I had reached the top of the staircase. "Eloise?"

There was the screaming, but nothing else that I could hear above it.

"Finn?" I called again, gripping the banister.

"Fine!" I heard the word bellowed from somewhere downstairs.

"Oh, thank God," I whispered, clutching my chest with relief at the sound of my friend's voice. I hadn't even realized how anxious I had become at his silence. "Where are you?" I yelled again.

"We're down b ... *fuck!*"

Eloise's scream had died abruptly at Finn's exclamation. Everything was terribly, utterly quiet.

"Finn?" I asked. My voice sounded meek and frightened.

My stomach turned, as I waited for a response. Only the dull groaning of the banister below my hand, straining under the considerable amount of weight I was putting on it, met my ears.

I swallowed back against an upsurge of bile. *Do you want to know what it feels like to die?*

The skin under my scalp ached with pressure, and I pinched my fingers together painfully. *What does it matter now?* I reached up for the scarf, removing the pins keeping it in place. Next the wig, then the wig cap.

Once my scalp was free of its coverings, the pressure, whilst still there, seemed to have lessened considerably. I didn't need to pull.

The first step was hard, but I took it quickly. If Finn needed me, wherever he was, I would be there.

"Finn!" I called with more strength to my voice, once I had reached the bottom of the stairs. There was still no answer. Not having a light, I could only see a short way in front of me. There were enough windows in this main part of the house for the moon to provide some guidance, though it cast everything into shadow. The old house sounded like a ship at sea as I walked, creaking and groaning as if under an immense pressure.

I navigated a labyrinth of hallways, finally coming out into the windowed corridor that led to Sam's old study.

I saw the paintings of the bluebonnet girl, and the beautiful young woman on the swing. It was too dark to make them out clearly, but my eyes lingered for a while on the second one. It made me think of cherry blossoms and springtime, of love and hope; things that seemed so foreign and unattainable now.

I walked on, my head turning automatically to the row of windows and the courtyard beyond. There was movement.

I stood frozen in place, watching the moonlit scene. Something, or someone, was in front of the stone fountain. It trembled as I walked. Getting closer to the window, I saw that it was Eloise, kneeling in the snow with her face buried in her hands. I rapped the window and called out, trying to get her attention, to get her to come back inside without having to go out into the night myself.

She didn't look back, or do anything to acknowledge she had heard me. I took a step back, scanning the courtyard for Finn, my heart in my throat. Blessedly, I caught sight of him standing in one corner, across from where Eloise was kneeling. He was gesturing with his arms, was saying something to her, but I couldn't see his face to be able to tell for sure. I did notice the gleam of metal from the pistol he held. *He must've retrieved it from the table in the hallway when he had been running after Eloise*, I thought.

I took a deep breath, bracing myself for what I was going to do next. I didn't want to experience any more of this nightmare, didn't want to think about whatever was lurking out there. For Finn, I'd walk through Hell itself.

CHAPTER TEN

"What is she doing?" I whispered. I had navigated around to the side of the courtyard to the exterior door closest to Finn. He had visibly tensed when I'd pushed it open a fraction, alert for any sign of an attack.

Upon turning to see it was me, his shoulders had dropped. In answer to my whispered question, he only put his arm out, and motioned with his hand for me to remain inside. I shook my head, mouthing the words *not without you*, though I doubted he would be able to make them out in the darkness.

Careful to move as quietly as possible, I opened the door fully until it was touching the wall behind it, then used my foot to wedge a rug mat underneath it, to prevent it closing behind me. I wanted to provide us an easy option of escape, should we need it.

I stepped out onto the snow once again, my feet still only in socks. The air felt bitingly cold but strangely refreshing on my exposed scalp. It caused me to shiver. Finn was shaking his head but didn't make a move to try to stop me from coming out. Instead, he faced front again, looking at the hunched, trembling form of Eloise. I didn't say anything else until I was right next to him, my shoulder brushing his arm.

"Can't we just … carry her inside?" My eyes scanned the skies, though I was sure I would be able to hear the spine-chilling beat of wings before I saw the thing, whatever it was. I didn't feel the least bit self-conscious, knowing Finn could see me, the *real* me, without any attempt at disguise. *What had I been so afraid of before? It's just hair, just skin, just superficial.* What we were facing now, tonight, *that* warranted actual fear. That was a true threat. And the people here, this house, the man standing beside me, those were the things that mattered … the *only* things that mattered to me. My apartment, my job as a waitress at a chain restaurant downtown, I never realized how unimportant those things were … until now.

The sound of Finn exhaling next to me pulled me from my thoughts. "If I even get close to her, she starts that fuckin' screaming again. I don't want her drawing attention to us, but I don't really know what else to do. I can't just leave her out here, and she doesn't pay any attention when I try to whisper to her." He shrugged in resignation. "I guess there's really no choice. I'll have to try my best to keep her quiet while I drag her back inside. What else can I do?" he repeated. "We can't stay here."

"Wait." I reached up to put my hand on his shoulder. "Let me try to approach her. I'm a little less … imposing than you are."

Finn shook his head. "No, I—"

But I didn't give him the chance to argue the point. I was already creeping toward the fountain, behind which Eloise was on her knees in the snow. I could feel the brush of Finn's fingertips at my back as he reached for me, but I had moved quickly enough that he was unable to grasp on to anything.

Keeping my eyes on the pitiful, trembling form of Eloise, I continued forward, marveling at the fact my feet seemed to make no sound upon the snow. As I drew nearer to her, I slowed, licking my wind-chapped lips. I was struggling to ignore my body's glaring command to run for shelter.

"Eloise," I whispered, as gently as I could, when I was close enough to reach out and touch her. Closing my eyes tight, I braced myself for the inevitable scream. When it didn't come, I let out my breath and opened my eyes again.

Eloise was looking up at me, her wide eyes scanning my face and up to my real, sweat-drenched hair. She blinked at the sight of it but gave no other acknowledgement that it was anything strange.

I knelt down, so that I was at eye-level with her. "Come with me," I whispered, forcing my cracked lips to spread into what I hoped was a reassuring smile.

She opened her mouth, but no sound came out. Her lips trembled, and she turned her eyes toward the stone fountain. Mouth still agape, she reached up with one arm to point directly at the stone, a look of unfiltered terror upon her face.

My skin prickled all over, as I followed her gaze with mine. I hadn't really looked at the *angel* in years, but it was just as terrifying as I remembered. The chiseled form loomed over me. It stood at least eight or nine feet tall, its large wings folded eternally at its back, but the worst thing about it was its face.

The brow was furrowed, the eyes deeply set like a hawk's. What I really found unsettling was that it looked almost human. It was as if something had tried to disguise itself as a human but had not quite succeeded. The nose was sunken rather than protruding, giving the face an almost skull-like appearance. Its mouth jutted out, like a deformed beak, bony and rounded. The strange jaws culminated into a grim, straight line.

Its eyes were intense and stern, expertly carved, making them seem as though they truly *were* watching.

The color of the statue, slate gray, only added to its melancholy appearance. It wasn't something I enjoyed looking at by any means, but seeing it, still and unmoving in the snow, relieved me of some ridiculous notion I'd been trying hard to ignore.

I looked back at Eloise. Her face was disconcertingly still. She wasn't pointing any longer, but her eyes remained fixed on the fountain statue. I crept closer, blocking her view as I positioned myself between her and the thing she was so focused on.

I could see the pale, circular moon reflected in the unshed tears glossing her eyes. Then, something else. A strangled sound escaped her throat. There was the grinding noise of movement just behind me. In Eloise's eyes, I could see the reflection of something large, and dark, spreading its ... wings.

I turned my head slowly, ever so slowly, to look over my shoulder. One enormous, smooth stone wing blocked my view of the moon completely. My mouth went dry, I could not even scream. Eloise let out a strange, whimpering laughter.

The wing flexed. It looked leathery, like that of a bat. I couldn't move, couldn't look away. It wasn't possible. *It wasn't possible.*

There was more of the grinding noise I had heard before, like stone against stone. Then, the wing came down sharply, cutting through the air, to beat once, twice. Wind surged over me at the movement, chilling me to the bone. The statue … the *thing*, began to rise. I could see the length of its tall, stone body as it started to ascend. I was going to die. *Like this.*

"What the fuck!" Finn's words echoed my thoughts. The sound of his voice rattled me enough to break through my fear-induced stupor.

I moved around beside Eloise, putting an arm over her trembling shoulders. We had to get away. It didn't matter that something *impossible* was happening, The only thing I needed to do right now was to get us inside, where it was safe.

I heard the beating wings of the thing, and reflexively looked up. The eyes, under the low, furrowed brow, were fixed on mine. They were intense and animalistic, like an eagle watching a field mouse. I could feel the blood draining from my face to pool in my limbs, urging me to run. Instead, I dropped down to lie flat on my belly, pushing Eloise hard with my arm to force her to do the same. I put my head down too, covering the back of it with my hands, as though it would matter. The memory of what this thing had done to Lucas, to Paul, to David, of the way it had so easily torn through their flesh, tormented me. A warm wetness soaked through my clothes, but I hardly registered the fact that I had urinated. All I felt, was fear.

I heard the wings beating again. My face contorted into a grimace against the snow. There was a swooping sound high above me, then another, closer … and another, closer yet … then, a gunshot. *A gunshot.*

I remembered what Finn had said earlier, about the sound of a bullet ricocheting off something hard when he was sure he had hit the thing flying above us. What chance did a pistol have against solid granite? The swooshing stopped. Instead, there was the sound of beating wings again, but they were moving away from me. Another shot rang out. *No, Finn.*

I scrambled to my feet, slipping on the hard snow as my body began to regain feeling. Everything burned as circulation made a sluggish return to my extremities. My movements were slow, clumsy.

I looked up to see my worst fear realized. The thing was posed to dive, its strangely humanoid legs pointed almost gracefully at the toes. It was moving directly at Finn.

Another shot rang out, at the same time I cried, "No!" at the very top of my lungs.

My breath was ragged, heartbeat frantic as the creature descended. Its wings had engulfed Finn before it had even landed. I heard the sound of tearing flesh, of blood spilling onto snow.

"*No!*" I could taste blood as the ferocity of my scream tore at my throat. I did not feel the pain, immune to everything but what had happened to Finn. Time seemed to move in slow motion, yet I could not do anything to stop what was happening. Finn's body fell without a sound, his neck bent sideways at an unnatural angle. The creature hunched toward him, then was lifting him in the air as it flew. There was the sound of breaking bone, as Finn's body was crushed in its large hands, like he was nothing more substantial than soft clay. The noise twisted at my insides. My body felt hot all over, despite the frigid night, and something snapped in my brain, like an overstretched rubber band.

I watched with unblinking eyes as the thing carried Finn's body over to the fountain, where the large basin had been centered atop the base. The pulpy mass of bones and skin in the gargoyle's hands was not my friend. Finn was gone, but I could feel him all around me, as though in the shock of the moment, his soul had lingered, not realizing yet that it had been wrenched from his body. That was ridiculous, I knew, but it felt real to me, his presence.

The thing landed softly upon the snow, its wings stretched out to either side of its stone body. It bent to put the flesh it carried into the large basin. It stood then, resuming its original pose, its wings tucking in at its back as it poured liquid from the basin into the fountain base. Instead of water though, thick, crimson blood was flowing over the stone. Eloise screamed.

CHAPTER ELEVEN: *THEM*

The blood of the mother within the blood of the son. She is here, because he is here. They are us. Our body stretches, accommodating all our parts as they fuse seamlessly. We will not let another go, will not risk losing one of our own. More of the blood, we chant.

Chapter Twelve

The fountain was just a fountain. I clenched my fists, punching it with all the strength in my trembling body. My knuckles bruised and bled until I couldn't feel them anymore. Still, I kept hitting, but the thing was inanimate.

Eloise was screaming, on her knees rocking back and forth. I was yelling too, mostly curses and inhuman growls. We were each experiencing our own brand of psychological breakdown.

I heard a cracking sound as my fist made another contact with the stone. My middle finger dangled limply, and I was no longer able to bend it into my palm. Blood ran from its base to its tip, dripping onto the snow at my feet. Red on white.

A noise behind me caused me to turn. Aunt Theodora was waddling out from the house. She was smiling in a friendly, nonchalant way, despite the hellish noises issuing from both myself and her daughter, Eloise.

"Hello, dear," she said as she approached me.

I only looked at her, my lower jaw shaking so hard that my teeth clashed together.

"Don't be sad. I think he's the model car, upstairs in his bedroom. I heard its little tires spinning when I passed by there. Anyway, he's something here, Finn. Alice too, we're so happy to have her back."

"What are you talking about?" I managed, though my pronunciation was garbled and strange.

"What I told you, this house holds onto us. I felt it when I died, just there." She gestured to a dark corner at one side of the courtyard. "I was not my body anymore, I was like air rising, rising.

But I felt myself being pulled back to this place, like a magnetic force I couldn't break from. I attached to the thing I was most attracted to, my own body. I had been in it so long, you see, but I should have chosen something else, something permanently *here* in this house, like my sister Gigi chose the cherub, Paul, the piano, and Finn, the model car." She looked at the fountain, where blood was still running in the place of water. "We can feel it, the blood. It connects us, I think, although I'm not as integrated as the others."

"Finn's dead." The words felt stale on my tongue, dry and shriveled.

"The house couldn't risk losing him, it had already missed out on Alice. She didn't die here, she died in the hospital, so there was no way for the house to pull her into something. Finn was the only connection it had left to get her blood here with us. So the house killed him, to save him, to keep him here, and her, Alice, where they belong. Our family, together and whole."

I couldn't process what she was trying to tell me. Family members who died here were sucked back into some object in the house? I laughed, the sound coming out harsh and hollow.

"But we aren't whole, not quite yet," Aunt Theodora continued, ignoring my strange outburst. Her eyes flicked from me to Eloise then back again.

I heard stone grinding against stone just behind me.

"We still need Eloise, and you … well, you've always been family to us, dear." A smile cracked across her face.

There was the loud beat of wings, then … nothing.

CHAPTER THIRTEEN

I am floating, free of pain, free of body, free of my senses. I am lighter than air, soaring and ascending. The weightlessness is all I am aware of. There is no resistance at first, no gravity. Then, a warmth engulfs me, I feel myself as pure light, only energy. I hesitate.

Something pulls at me, tugging me like a magnet. I think of the Ferguson house, of the people I had known there. The pull becomes stronger. I think of Sam and Alice, of Aunt Theodora and ... Finn. I think of, or rather, I feel the house itself. An image of the portrait detailing the woman in the cherry blossoms is all around me. I am pulled there so forcefully I am like a gust. Then I am perched on a swing, the scent of cherry blossoms washes over me. The air is as fresh as springtime, clean and brand new. I have hair, thick and long, and a beautiful lavender dress. I am looking out into the courtyard.

Eloise's body is in the arms of the gargoyle, being manipulated into the basin. She does not feel pain, I know. As soon as her blood begins to flow to the base, I can feel it coursing through the ground and roots, through the pipes and bricks of the manor, through me. I can feel Finn too, and through him, Alice. I can feel Sam, as well, Paul and David ... and others, so many others, connected as one through the blood. Family. They are me. I am home. I am them.

ABOUT THE AUTHOR

Erica Schaef is a fan of all things horror and loves to write her own stories in that genre. She is an Affiliate Writer member of the Horror Writers Association. Her work has been featured in a variety of journals, magazines, audio productions, and anthologies. She lives in rural Tennessee with her husband and two wild children.

About the Illustrator

Elizabeth Leggett is a Hugo award-winning illustrator whose work focuses on soulful, human moments-in-time that combine ambiguous interpretation and curiosity with realism.

Much to her mother's dismay, she viewed her mother's whitewashed walls as perfectly good canvasses so she believes it is safe to say that she has been an artist her whole life! Her first published work was in the Halifax County Arts Council poetry and illustration collection. If she remembers correctly, she was not yet in double digits yet, but she might be wrong about that. Her first paying gig was painting other students' tennis shoes in high school.

In 2012, she ended a long fallow period by creating a full seventy-eight card tarot in a single year. From there, she transitioned into freelance illustration. Her clients represent a broad range of outlets, from multiple Hugo award winning *Lightspeed Magazine* to multiple Lambda Literary winner, Lethe Press. She was honored to be chosen to art direct both *Women Destroy Fantasy* and *Queers Destroy Science Fiction*, both under the Lightspeed banner.

Elizabeth, her husband, and their typically atypical cats, live in New Mexico. She suggests if you ever visit the state, look up. The skies are absolutely spectacular!

ACKNOWLEDGEMENTS

Thank you to my husband, Sawyer, for supporting me in whatever I do.

Thank you to my mom for her unconditional love and boundless creativity.

Thank you to my dad, for always encouraging me.

Thank you to my grandparents, for having the best stories to tell me when I was young.

Thank you to my sister, Staci, who is my long-suffering beta-reader, for her patience and care.

Thank you to everyone at Brigids Gate for the time and attention you have given my story.

Lastly, thank you reader, for having chosen this book. I hope you enjoyed it!

CONTENT WARNINGS

Death
Cancer
Gore
Mental Illness

MORE FROM BRIGIDS GATE PRESS

A Quaint and Curious Volume of Gothic Tales; 23 stories of madness, pain, ghosts, curses, unspoken secrets, greed, murder, and one of the creepiest collections of dolls ever. Ranging from traditional gothic themes to more modern tropes, this anthology is sure to please the reader ... and send a cold shiver or two down their spine.

So, come on in; enter the parlor, find a place by the fire, and experience the beautiful, dark, and occasionally heartbreaking stories told by the authors. The editor, Alex Woodroe, has passionately and carefully curated a powerful volume of stories, written by an amazing and diverse group of contemporary women writers.

Tyler Torrence has inherited his late grandfather's house, a home filled with bad memories and nightmares from his childhood. He returns hoping to learn the truth of his grandfather's secrets, especially the secret of the 'impossible bottles' and what lay beyond the black door. The door through which he was never allowed to enter as a child.

But returning to the house is a mistake. It doesn't take long for Tyler to realize the hold the house has over him, and that he is a prisoner of the ancestral curse that claimed his grandfather. Now he must fight to break the curse before it claims him and his son.

Betrayal brings grave ending to a noble bloodline. Forced to flee, its sole surviving heir is spared this fate by the timely intervention of a haunter of the wilds. In his charge, the maiden embraces the lore of the dark arts and rises to become the watch-keep of the woods. As decades pass, with her legend growing, the 'witch of root and earth' weaves subtle deceits in a tangled web of vengeance.

But will there be a fairy tale ending, or will poisoned legacies and pacts with dark forces see ambition unravel in her relentless pursuit of power?

Bloody, and brilliantly realised, Baird's dark fantasy nightmare spins a lavish tale of dread, desire, and fantastical fury.

Stewartville. A town living in the shadow of the prisons that drive its economy. Haunted by the ghosts of its past. Cursed by the dark secrets hidden beneath. A town so entwined with the prisons waiting outside the city limits that it's impossible to imagine one without the other, or to ever imagine escaping either.

When a teenage boy digs into the history of the town, he discovers a tunnel system beneath Stewartville, passageways filled with dark secrets. Secrets leading not to freedom, but to unrelenting terror.

Stewartville. Where the convicts aren't the only prisoners.